Hugh Haliburton

In Scottish Fields

Hugh Haliburton

In Scottish Fields

ISBN/EAN: 9783337232177

Printed in Europe, USA, Canada, Australia, Japan

Cover: Foto ©Andreas Hilbeck / pixelio.de

More available books at **www.hansebooks.com**

IN SCOTTISH FIELDS

In Scottish Fields

BY

HUGH HALIBURTON

AUTHOR OF "HORACE IN HOMESPUN," "FOR PUIR AULD SCOTLAND'S SAKE"

WILLIAM PATERSON & CO.
LOVELL'S COURT, PATERNOSTER ROW
LONDON
1890

PREFACE.

THE present collection of essays stands to its predecessor, *For Puir Auld Scotland's Sake*, in the relation of a second series. The general subject is continued, and various aspects of Scottish rural and literary life are presented in such a way as, it is hoped, may prove not uninteresting even to English readers.

A small proportion of Scottish words and phrases, recommended either by their raciness or their expressiveness, has been introduced into the text, and explained in a short glossary at the end of the book.

The paper on *Our Earlier Burns* is a popular treatment of the subject, and

was written before the publication, by the
Scottish Text Society, of Sheriff Mackay's
scholarly and genial estimate of William
Dunbar.   An apology to the student of
early Scottish forms is perhaps due for
daring to modernise an old Makkar.

Most of the papers in this collection are,
by kind permission, reproduced from the
Scotsman, some from the *Scots Observer*,
and one from *Good Words*.   To the editors
and proprietors of these periodicals due ac-
knowledgment of the author's indebtedness
is here gratefully made.

CONTENTS.

IN SCOTTISH FIELDS.

HOLY FAIRS.

" I suld at the fairs be found,
New faces to spy ;
At plays and at *preachings*
And pilgrimages great."
—DUNBAR.

THE nineteenth century has proved, in the language of curlers, a *hogscore* to not a few old Scottish customs. Transmitted from a distant past, they have been arrested at this fateful boundary, and withdrawn for ever from the rink of time. They have now scarcely more than an antiquarian interest. Of those ancient customs the celebration of the Holy Fair was one. For at least two and a half centuries it was a familiar part of the popular religious life in this end of the island; it lost its good name, justly or unjustly, and perhaps a little of both, towards the close of last century; failed to retrieve it in the two genera-

A

tions that succeeded; and may now be regarded
as extinct, beyond all hope of revival. It is as
dead as the Miracle Play. If some little
upland hamlet, here and, at a long interval,
there, be still fitfully brightened by its presence,
the phenomenon, though interesting in a way,
is of no vital significance; it is a mere curiosity,
like the Passion Play at Ober-Ammergau.
Has it deserved to die? That we venture to
doubt. Undeniably, whatever evil to the public
morals it might ultimately have done, it was productive of much good. The sanction of a whole
nation, lay and clerical, continued for many years,
is proof of its respectability and guarantee
of its good. It was a good institution initially,
and subsequently till near the close; but we
have the Laureate's authority that a good
custom may corrupt the world. It was, it
must be confessed, made the means of corrup-
tion. It was taken possession of by Fun, and
Superstition, and Hypocrisy, on the testimony
of Burns, a keen observer of both men and
movements. His exposure, while immortalis-
ing it in the corrupt stage of its existence,
killed instead of reforming it. The result of
his satire is, perhaps, to be regretted. It did
good, if death be better than incurable disease.
But reform at the hands of an enlightened
and pious clergy would have been best. The
institution was essentially good in its aims;

its capabilities were elastic, and were unex-
hausted. Brought into healthy harmony with
the spirit of the age, the Holy Fair might
have been in existence still—a popular and
beneficial agency in the religious life of Scotland. Under wise guidance and fostering
control, it might have had a development in
the Church proportional in some degree to
the development of the miracle play in the
theatre. The paganism of civilised Greece
was wiser in its generation, in so far as it
sought to surround its religious practice with
the refining and liberalising influences of external nature.

The Holy Fair has disappeared within the
memory of men still living. Familiar to their
youth as a common summer festival, more or
less loosely connected with religion, it is now to
their old age a faint and far-off recollection.
Ostensibly it was a gathering of Christians
convoked at some rural central spot for the
purpose of religious exercises, preparatory to a
celebration of the Lord's Supper. The religious
exercises took place in the open air, and were
continued without intermission throughout the
day, while the more sacred ordinance of the
sacrament was dispensed to communicants,
coming and retiring in relays, under the roof
of the little adjoining church. The institution
as thus defined was as old, at least, as the reign

of the first Charles. Whatever its origin, it was at length appropriated by the Protestants, and by-and-by became associated in the popular mind with Presbyterianism and the principles of Dissent. This result was brought about in the dark years of prelacy and persecution, when men were driven from the kirk to the canopy of heaven for the freedom of a mode of worship which the law denied to them under a consecrated roof. The conventicle, in the lown glen or on the lone hillside, may not have been the origin of the religious gathering known in later times as the Holy Fair, but it certainly gave the practice of assembling in the open air for devotional purposes the impetus which brought it within measurable reach of our own day. A time at last arrived when the obnoxious restrictive laws were removed, and religious liberty was allowed. It was no longer necessary to meet by stealth, and plant sentinels to secure uninterrupted worship; and Holy Fairs held among the snows of winter vanished from the wildernesses of Scotland. From being a painful necessity of free religious existence they became a species of voluntary festival or sacred holiday, attendance at which was no test of the robustness of religious character. The laxest might attend, and the most rigidly righteous might stay away. The custom was maintained in many districts as a memento of the old

Covenanting times; much in the same way as the ancient Israelites inaugurated the joyous Feast of Tabernacles, in remembrance of the painful wanderings of their forefathers in the desert.

If we mistake not, the first authentic Holy Fair in Scottish historical record is of date 1630. But there can be little doubt that large religious meetings in the open air were held more or less statedly in the country when Roman Catholicism was supreme, and a rival religion was undreamt of. The clergy in the Middle Ages made it a point to gratify popular instincts as far as the gratification of them was consistent with the dignity, or at least the supremacy, of the Church, and generally to associate religious ordinances and observances with secular employments and pastimes. The modern drama was founded and fostered up to a certain period in its development by the Church; holidays were of priestly appointment and had Papal sanction; secular fairs and markets were instituted and upheld under the patronage of saints. Evidence of this patronage is still broadcast over Protestant Scotland. St Luke and St John are still supposed to preside over many a Scottish market. They have now only the barren honour of naming the market; but doubtless in the good old times they levied, in the persons of their priestly representatives, certain tolls and taxes, in kind or in coin, in return for the benefit of their patronage. The advantages secured to themselves by the clergy in ministering to the popular instincts which seek after variety and sociality, by permitting and directing the practice of what may be called by anticipation Holy Fairs, were a larger and more intimate influence over the people, a more permanent popularity, and a relaxation from the pressure of monotony and the routine of monastic life. It may be that our modern clergy keep too much aloof from the pastimes and social gatherings of the people, giving themselves ostensibly too much up to spiritual work. But the manifestation of a few more mundane instincts, and a wider practical humanity than they are generally in the habit of showing, would, if accompanied by a spirit of sincerity and fraternal equality, produce a double benefit in the creation of a sound and sensible sympathy between pastor and people. The cricket field, the theatre, the curling pond, rural games, dancing—in themselves, and generally in the way in which they are now conducted, innocent and healthful means of exercise and intercourse —are almost wholly abandoned by our modern clergy. No thoughtful person will deny that in this abandonment of practices and customs which are too firmly rooted in human nature to be eradicated, the clergy are neglecting the use of agencies at once legitimate and powerful, and which are capable at the same time of effecting a large increase of the social and moral as well as physical welfare of the community. Their predecessors of the Middle Ages knew better, or were more courageous in their knowledge. The Protestant minister might well take a leaf or two, even yet, from the book of the Roman Catholic priest—more especially the minister who protests against Rome and *dissents* from every place else.

Up to this point we are to be understood as referring rather to the thing named than to the name by which it was known. The expression Holy Fair was probably never generally applied to the institution which it designates till the satire of Burns spread it broadcast over the country. Tent-preaching was, perhaps, the more common appellative. Holy Fair may, or may not, have been originally an irreverent application, but there is no doubt the unqualified word *Fair* was long ago used to describe a public solemnity of a ceremonial nature. In the verses of the old Scottish "Makkars," for instance, we read of funeral fairs, as the grim festivities attending the obsequies of a departed chieftain were called. One has probably no incorrect notion of the nature of those festivities from Scott's account of the fair at Coningsburgh Castle, on the occasion of the supposed death

of Athelstane, as recorded in the romance of
" Ivanhoe," chapter forty-first. Scott speaks of
those festivities, which included eating and
drinking, playing and chanting, and even jug-
gling and jesting, as doubtless rude, but still as
natural as they were rude. " If sorrow was
thirsty," he says, "there was drink; if hungry,
there was food; if it sunk down upon and
saddened the heart, here were the means supplied of mirth, or at least of amusement. Nor
did the mourners scorn to avail themselves of
those means of consolation, although every now
and then, as if suddenly recollecting the cause
which had brought them together, the men
groaned in unison, while the females, of whom
many were present, raised up their voices and
shrieked for very woe." This was the funeral
fair; the obsequies proper, meanwhile, were being
conducted by the priests in the presence of the
body, while the next of kin lamented in dreary
elegies the mortality of man. From this, and
kindred uses of the word, *Fair* is obviously of
Latin derivation, and signified a festival of some
sort or other. If the word could be applied
to the celebration of funeral rites continued
between death and burial, its transference to the
performance of sacramental rites and services
at social gatherings in the open air was easy
and almost unavoidable.

In Ayrshire, and the south-western districts

of Scotland generally, "Holy Fair" may have been the popular designation of those gatherings; but elsewhere in Scotland, and notably in the midlands, the "preaching," or more fully "tent-preaching," was the expression in current use. The tent, from which the preaching was made, requires a little explanation. It was not of canvas, or cloth of any kind, but of wood, usually painted black, occasionally of a dull white, and correctly enough described as a box supported on four legs some three or four feet from the ground, and provided with a projecting awning, or rather sounding-board, over the opening in front, from which the clergyman addressed the congregations and directed the religious exercises. The comparison may be profane, and no doubt is so in a classical sense, but the ecclesiastical tent, which was the central point of the Holy Fair, resembled nothing so much as the familiar box from which the dramatic show of Punch and Judy still happily continues to be displayed, to the delectation and instruction of the British youth of all ages. The "holy door," as Burns irreverently calls it, which gave admission to the tent, was "speeled," or scaled, by a short flight of three or four steps placed against one of the sides of the wooden structure. As the preaching went on from early forenoon till nearly nightfall, without other intermission than ministerial praying and congregational singing, there was necessarily a succession of preachers ; "the guard was continually being relieved," to adopt the language of Burns, and the tent from time to time "changed its voice," in more senses than one.

It is remarkable that Scott, who had a keen eye for social phenomena as illustrative of national character, and inimitable skill in handling them for fictional purposes, has neglected to utilise a subject so inviting as the institution of the Holy Fair. In "Old Mortality" he has treated with impressive force the sterner aspect of the persecuted conventicle, and given a few flying glimpses, principally in the report of Cuddy Headrigg and the conduct of that worthy's mother Mause, of the comic side which, perhaps, every social subject presents to the eye of the humorist. Elsewhere, in the calmly entrancing scenes of "The Abbot," he has portrayed the fun and frolic of the secular fair, as exemplified on the level shore of lowland Loch Leven. But he has nowhere, in the rich series of his Scottish romances, delineated that combination of the conventicle and the village *fête* which, in varying proportions, constituted the Holy Fair. The subject could hardly have escaped his notice as a living part in the system of things religious in the midst of which he lived. And, in any case, he was conversant with Burns' treatment of the theme. It may

have been that he was deterred from dealing
with the subject by the acrimonious hostility
which sprang up on the presentation of Burns'
picture, and which refused to recognise in that
picture a just, or even partially true, exposure
of the features of the Holy Fair of his day.
The bitterness of the opposition to Burns'
satire was well known to Scott ; it was, indeed,
a very adequate specimen of the very similar
criticism with which his own representation of
the Covenanters was afterwards assailed. And
yet it cannot be denied that the Holy Fair had
other aspects than the humorous, hypocritical,
and superstitious aspects to which Burns
restricted his burin. Genuine religion and the
kindly social feeling of true humanity were not
seldom in the camp of which fun, superstition,
and hypocrisy were, in greater or less admixture,
the inevitable sutlers. Perhaps Scott's sympathy was, upon the whole, with Burns' mode
of treatment ; and as Burns had exhausted, by
a few masterly strokes, those aspects of the
case which, on this supposition, recommended
themselves to the kindred artistic eye of Scott,
the novelist was content to be anticipated by
the poet, and to leave the subject in the entire
possession of the latter. There is just this to
object to the theory here advanced, that Scott
not infrequently undertook, without improving,
subjects which had already received ample

treatment at the hands of the elder masters; but it is sufficient to meet this objection with the well-known fact that Scott—by no means sensitive to literary criticism—was still by natural disposition a man of peace, a satirist only in the Chaucerian sense, and therefore inclined to avoid subjects which it was impossible to handle freely, and according to the dictates of what one may call his artistic conscience, without incurring the personal discomfort of party animosity, always fiercest when directed by a spirit of fanaticism. The Holy Fair was in his day such a subject.

But it is time to pass from this rambling disquisition on the origin and history of the Holy Fair, and to offer a description of the more interesting features of that now, alas! defunct institution as they yet linger in the writer's early recollection. And yet, before finally parting from the subject of origin, we are tempted here to put on record three different versions of the matter from as many individuals living in the same district, who were interrogated on the point. "What began tent-preachin', quo' ye?" queried auld Tammas, as he raised the lid of his tin snuff-box. "What ither than the heat o' the kirk, an' aiblins the musty smell o't? The minister bood (*behoved*) to ca' oot his flock to the green pastures an' the quate watters, as Dawvid says, or swite i' the poopit, wi' sma' pleasure to himsel' an' nae profit to his people, wha wad a' be sleepin'!" But tent-preaching did not last all through the heat of summer. "Na," said Tammas, "that *wad* be a carnal indulgence atweel!" Old Andro's theory was that the practice was meant to commemorate Covenanting times, "when the Lord's people campit i' the gressy wilderness, like a covey o' huntit paitricks. It was richt to call to mind the mainner o' life o' oor forebears. It should mak' us thankfu' for wa's an' ruifs, and an unmolestit ministry." A different opinion was at once offered by auld Eppie. "It was for faut o' kirks, an' sma' kirks. Folk wad gang ten or twal miles i' my green days to hear a preachin', an' think it but a Sabbath day's journey. There were fewer ministers than, an' they were mair thocht o'. Aiblins they better deserved it. An' you maun mind when a curn o' them cam' to assist at the Sacrament there were nae young preachers to tak' their place at hame. Their folk juist gade wi' them, or steyed at hame an' keepit kirk i' their ain kitchens. And if three or fowre congregations met thegither, whaur was the sma' kirk to haud them? They were obleeged to tak' the fields for't." The possible explanations of the origin of the custom are now, with those just reported, pretty well exhausted.

The Holy Fair was of annual observance in

the district where it had become established—
some pastoral braeside or valley nook within
easy reach of a rural church. In some of the
larger villages, or where no very convenient
place of assembly was to be had in the adjoining fields, resort was made to the churchyard,
the people finding bottom-room on the table
gravestones and grassy mounds of the sacred
enclosure. Perhaps the most picturesque and
most popular site for a Holy Fair was among
solitary hills near a little hamlet, six or eight
miles from a circle of six or eight villages and
similar hamlets, with, it might be, a provincial
town of some pretensions, and a population of
four or five thousand, as the principal point in
the circumference. Some of our readers will
probably know of some such place among the
Ayrshire hills or on the sunny side of the more
central Ochils. The day selected was commonly
a Sunday in July or the early part of August.
Mauchline Holy Fair, which has attained such
notoriety, and which so many have refused as a
type of the Holy Fairs of their experience, was
held in the churchyard on an early Sunday in
August. Either of these months gave the
advantages of a long day and, except in very
abnormal seasons, fine weather. People were
thus allowed to attend in comfort from far and
wide. The time selected was, besides, peculiarly suitable for the country folks resident in

the neighbourhood, occurring as it did before
the labours of the corn harvest were required.
Of course, the occasion of the tent-preaching
was the celebration of the more impressive
Sacrament, and was preceded on a secular day
in the previous week by a solemn fast. But
farm folk could not afford a day in harvest for
the fast. It must be remembered that in those
days fasts preceding the Sacrament were kept
as strictly as Sabbaths. No work was permitted ;
whistling was sinful ; to cut a stick in a thicket
or a hedge was deserving in an especial manner
the pains which the Shorter Catechism declares
every sin deserves. And everybody put on his
black clothes, just as on a Sabbath day. The
day was withheld from secular work with Jewish
rigidity.

The Sacrament of the Lord's Supper, which
was the prime motive of the religious gathering
at a Holy Fair, was dispensed not to the many,
unless when special arrangements for the purpose were made, but to the few—it was not for
the strangers, "all and some," but for local
communicants, and for ministers and elders from
a distance of established reputation. But all,
without distinction of character, sheep and goats
alike, were permitted to mix indiscriminately
around the tent to listen at will to the sermons
and addresses and take part in the social worship on the open platform of nature, rendered

doubly attractive in the fine summer weather by the beauty of blooming broom and the fragrance of aromatic herbs and flowers in the full-grown grass. The freedom of conduct which the gathering permitted was a great cause of its popularity, as it was also in some instances the inlet for its abuse. The gathering was in effect a holiday recreation, the religious nature of which in no ways detracted from, but rather sanctioned, its enjoyment by the masses. It afforded a much-desiderated means of seeing friends and society generally. Trysts were made, especially between the sexes, weeks and weeks before the day came round. The day was long looked forward to, always hopefully. Elders, separated from each other by the width of a parish or twain, had their annual reunions on the tent green: they interchanged news with their snuff-boxes, sniffed vigorously at the faintest taint of heresy in the homily of some suspected preacher, discussed predestination or the awful doctrine of infant damnation over a bap and a bottle of ale at refreshment time, or scoured away in long excursion, like the immortal Twa Dogs, among clerical anecdotes, parish gossip, and presbyterial scandal. Sisters met sisters, or brothers brothers, separated from each other for most of the year by the exigencies of service; they sat together, and sang from the same or from each other's Psalm-book, and found opportunity among less mortal thoughts to criticise their master or mistress's temper, their new acquaintance, and their former sweethearts. Elderly women came with their Bible, their bit of southernwood, and their house-key, to hear a favourite divine whom they had few opportunities of hearing, and whose ministra-tions were therefore more highly prized than a double dose of them weekly would probably have warranted. The day was looked back upon, sometimes regretfully. It was not in every case that Jock came to the preachings as Dan Chaucer went to Canterbury—" with full devout corage." Many a swankie came for the sake of fun and diversion. Some full-blooded halflins, their veins fired with oatmeal and the exercise of labour, came in plush vest and pearl buttons, with the buoyant expectation of a fight. A few were fully pre-determined for a " fill-up "—a boose of strong ale near nightfall.

A large attendance at the Holy Fair meant money for the particular kirk which authorised it. Each comer contributed on the average his penny. A pair had to "draw their tippence." The services conducted in the open never slacked. There was, as has been said, a succes-sion of preachers, all placed, i.e., beneficed, clergymen—with a chance probationer belonging to the locality, it might be. Burns humorously compares the tent to a spiritual sentry-box,

B

which was mounted from time to time by a
relieving sentinel. When the guard in occu-
pancy was long in being relieved, or had retired
too punctually or impatiently for his successor,
the interval was filled by congregational singing.
It was the only resource of the precentor, when
left in sole charge, as occasionally happened, of
the duties of the tent. He was sometimes
obliged to start a new psalm, having exhausted
the old one which the retiring minister had left
him with. The congregation sang on, heedless
of the character or appropriateness of the
sentiment. The volume of their united voices
varied as members came and went. The fringes
of the congregation, even at sermon time—
when they were most liable to rebuke for restlessness—were in a state of constant flux. A
step this way or that on the green sward
brought an individual within or beyond the
sacred pale. The proper season for joining or
withdrawing was during the psalm after the
sermon. The line was read by the "letter-gae,"
or precentor, before he sang it with the
congregation. This was a great convenience to
new-comers. It was read on the note which
kept the tune. But the "read" line, indeed,
was the custom at the ordinary service of praise.
There was great opposition to the innovation
of the "run" line, which is now, we should
think, in universal use. One argument of the

opposition party was that the blind could not participate in the holy service of praise if the run-line system of singing in the congregation were adopted. In one parish the representatives of this party appealed in confirmation of their argument to blind James Black. "Ou!" said the douce old man, whose Conservatism was of a different cast, "Ou! keep ye within the Psalms of David, an' ye'll no' put me aboot; ye'll no' want my help." James's implied objection was to the innovation of the Paraphrases.

The precentor, too, as well as the minister, needed relief. He had prudently arranged for this relief from the long and arduous labours of his part of the Holy Fair services. He had secured promises of help from neighbouring precentors. The precentors were aware of the mutual comparison to which their respective styles would be subjected. They came in for as keen a criticism indeed among rustic musical circles as the ministers themselves among connoisseurs of divinity and delivery. The precentor-in-chief, that is, the local precentor, would sometimes, when the day was well advanced, do some musical ploughman of his acquaintance the rare and highly-prized honour of giving up to him his post for the singing of a single psalm. The substitution of the amateur precentor was of great interest

to his friends and the juveniles of the congregation generally. How he would blush and roar,
with mingled abandonment and self-conscious-
ness! The Jennies tittered and looked askance,
and even douce elderly men, whose minds were
devoutly bent, would meditate episodically on
Jock's uncouth pronunciation. It was sometimes a trial, it may well be believed, for the
ploughman to read the line. He was rather
better at singing than at saying. But at both
his accent was full-flavoured. The bulls of
Bashan seemed to acquire a new terror as
buls of Bawshan. The bulls-of-Bashan class of
Psalms was what Jock, from natural temperament, revelled in. It would happen now and
again that the congregation, either from its size
or because of the wind that might be blowing
in gusts, or from a spirit of mischief abroad,
became unmanageable under the conduct of the
ploughman. They would run away with the
tune, or they would not take it up, or they
would change it in despite of all he could do.
The agony of his helplessness would take all
the stiffness out of Jock's collar. But when the
singing was fairly good, it was pleasant to hear
the tunes, old Covenanting favourites, Martyr-
dom, Bangor, Old Hundred, and York echoing
along the braes. These were among the time-
honoured traditional vehicles of praise, sacred
to the Scottish peasantry, both personally and

historically, and greatly affected by the Auld
Lichts and others who were impatient of State
intervention in the management of the Kirk's
affairs, and who seceded from the system of
patronage.

A favourite place among the Ochils for holding a tent-preaching was at the little hamlet of
Path-Struie. A kirk and a handful of cottages
beside it constituted the hamlet. They occupied
the top of the narrow ridge of elevated land
between the Chapel Burn and the Water of
May, just at the point where these two streams
unite in a sequestered but romantic haugh half-
way, on the summit of the broad Ochils,
between Lochleven and the Earn. The con-
fluent valleys of the Chapel and the May—the
latter still adorned in its lower course with the
birks which gave fragrance to the lines of
Malloch—as well as the haugh hollow in
which they meet, are bounded by steep grassy
banks, diversified here and there with bushes,
and broken by sheep-paths and terraces, favourable to a minute and leisurely survey of the
lovely scenery they both constitute and enclose.
Level plats extending from the water edge to
the bottom of the higher banks, lown places
over which the winds blow heedlessly, offered
an advantageous site for the tent, and ample
and convenient accommodation for the gathered
congregation. Brightened with the golden

blossoms of the broom and the virgin white
of the hawthorn—late, but nevertheless welcome,
is the visit of the May to Ochil glens!—and
tranquil with the hush of a blue Sabbath
morning in July, no better natural surroundings
for the celebration of a holy festival could be
found in Scotland. The churchyard is gloomy,
and rank with mortality; and one does not
know whether to attribute its selection as a site
for the Holy Fair to obtuseness, or to robustness of religious faith, on the part of our
ancestors. But at Path-Struie, under the conditions described, more than half of the sermon
lay to the preacher's hand on the banks and
braes around him; nature held out to him the
proofs of a benevolent providence, and the
cheerful symbols of life and immortality in the
joyous life of bird and insect, and the return of
its summer loveliness to the unforsaken glen.
Surely it is amid such surroundings as originally
gave their perfume and imagery to the Sermon
on the Mount that that priceless compendium
of Christian ethics, to produce its best and
fullest effect, should still be read in the ears of
men.

Intending worshippers—they were not all
such—entered by different accesses that part
of the grassy wild, which, by its proximity
to the tent, was tacitly known to be holy
ground. At different points on the outskirts

of the sacred area were placed, usually on
chairs draped in white, the *brodds*, or plates
for the offerings, mostly in copper, of the
congregation, while Black Bonnet, with or
wanting the "greedy glower" which Burns
detected in his countenance, sat or stood, hat
on head and hands behind him, patiently
guarding the accumulating treasure. There
might be three, or even four, brodds, one at
each of the airts. The tent stood in the haugh
or at the brae foot, and the people sat or lay on
the slopes near the broom bushes or among the
dry grass and rushes. The spoken sermon
at a tent-preaching was seldom the great
attraction of the gathering. At times, doubtless, there would be popular preachers who
would be followed even from the tent-green
into the adjoining kirk—the strangers to the
district going into the gallery, or *laft* as
it was called, while the communicants took
their places in the *laigh*, or low, kirk. But
even in the case of famous preachers there
was much to attract attention away from the
direct influence of the outdoor sermon. A jet
of wind or an unexpected turn of the preacher's
head might send the half of a sentence down
the glen, or a cow would venture near, and
set up a rival bellowing, though usually the
kye were carefully removed to distant pasture,
and it is but fair to Crummie to say that only

a loud-lunged son of thunder provoked her rivalry; or, lastly, and not to exhaust the list of counter attractions to the sermon, a pair of lovers, or a band of blackguard apprentices, might be descried coquetting with the sky-line on the heights overlooking the valley, or roaming in the hollow up the water side. The scenery itself was seductive. The look up the narrow winding valley was through a beautiful vista of pastoral slopes, the lines of which were drawn with charmingly delicate grace. The receding tints in the perspective of the valley were scarcely less delightful in their harmony. Here and there the slopes were hung with hedges, looking like fairy garlands in the distance. Less frequently, a light-leafed ash, or sisterhood of birches, mingling in the breeze their waving tresses, rose on the nearer heights in lovely outline against the sun-lighted sky.

The services commenced at eleven o'clock, and there was usually a big muster of hearers to start with. But people were coming and going all day long. They were drawn from an area extending from the point of assembly to a radial distance of eight or ten miles. Dunning, Abernethy, Kinross, and innumerable intermediate communities sent their contingents. Some drove to the fair in gigs or carts, the latter of all kinds of construction, from the

light *hurlie* to the heavy *cowp;* some were
mounted on ponies; but most rode on *shanksnaigie.* These last commonly took short cuts,
that frequently proved long cuts, over the hills
to the rendezvous. The pedestrians, chiefly
young men and women, when they had the
longer distance to travel, would set out from
home as early as eight in the morning. They
soon overtook or were joined by fellow-pilgrims,
until, as they approached their destination, they
were often a goodly company

> "Of sundry folk by aventure y-fall
> In fellowship."

Many such companies, converging on Path-
Struie from all the points of the compass,
gave to the roads in the vicinity of the hamlet
an appearance of unwonted bustle and variety.
The quiet country paths became as "throng"
as city thoroughfares. Burns has by no means
exaggerated :

> "For roads were clad, frae side to side,
>   Wi' mony a weary body,
>   In droves that day.
> "Here farmers gash, in ridin' graith,
>   Gaed hoddin' by their cotters ;
> There, swankies young, in braw braid claith,
>   Are springin' owre the gutters ;
> The lasses, skelpin' barefit, thrang,
>   In silks and scarlets glitter."

Friends and acquaintances were never done
hailing each other. There were hearty, demon-

strative forgatherings among the young. But
the sanctimonious Pharisee was there, too, with
his unsocial pride and manufactured face. And
there, too, were old staid canny neebour folk
belonging to the locality, quietly glad to see
the unwonted crowds, but preserving their
self-possession amid all the excitement with
the same simple ease with which auld Elspeth
carried her *beuk* and spray of *apple-ringie*, her
clean *hankie*, and her key.

The names of the officiating ministers were
known beforehand. Intimation of them was
made on the preceding fast-day. If the names
were popular, creditably or otherwise to their
owners—and, indeed, a touch of eccentricity, to
use no milder word, was rather a recommendation to a promiscuous audience—the effect might
be to induce a larger attendance. As a rule, the
local clergyman was assisted by three or four
of his Presbyterial brethren. If their churches
were in the neighbourhood, they were closed in
their absence, and their flocks, thus shut out of
their proper fold, for the most part accompanied
their shepherds to the wilderness. The ministers
were often as varied in their manner as in their
appearance. Any feature of gesture, pronunciation, or tone which differentiated the strangers
in the tent from the home-pastor was regarded
more or less as uncouth. Burns, if we remember
rightly, enumerates five officiating clergymen at

the Mauchline gathering—Moodie, Smith, wee
Miller, black Russell, and Peebles "frae the
water-foot"—and all typically different in their
styles and character. Representatives of very
much the same types were to be found at the
Path-Struie festival. Here was one with the
paradoxical gospel for which Dr Blair, of Edinburgh, suggested to the poet the memorable
expression—" Gude tidings of damnation ; " the
pulpit, or tent, delivery of such a gospel necessarily implied much " stampin' an' jumpin' " in
the lower limbs, with " eldritch squeals an' gestures " from the visible instruments of oratory.
Here was another with a message of "cauld
morality," uttered in such guarded monotones
and with such economy of gesture as thinned
the meeting—so that sometimes only the deaf
and the lame, with, of necessity, the precentor,
were left to the *Amen*. Here was a third with
more ingenuity in his analogies than common
sense in his arguments. A fourth had both
common sense and sound Christianity, preferring,
in the matter of delivery, the " gentle stream " of
Renwick to the thunders of Cameron. When a
decidedly unpopular preacher appeared at the
tent opening, many would rise, scarcely suppres-
sing words of displeasure the while, and, in the
most barefaced way, retire from the congregation. They could not sit for anger. A certain
Boänerges, who need not be nameless, seeing

he has been long unknown, was the special abomination — the word is a strong one — of shrill-voiced, wiry, wizened, old Bell Prap, who, as soon as the text was roared out, hastened to a convenient distance from which she could retort—"Yowt noo, Aiken! I ne'er likit a bane o' your buik : *ye* canna speak sma' bonny words like gude Maister Allan o' Cleish!"

The order of service was a psalm, a prayer, a reading from Scripture, a psalm, the sermon. Communicants then repaired to the church with the officiating clergyman, who there "fenced the tables" and dispensed "the elements." Meanwhile, on the tent ground a long psalm was being sung, another clergyman mounted the tent, and, after prayer, delivered the second sermon. In this way the outdoor services went on without a break till the shadows lengthened in the valley and the hour was seven, or even later. As many as four or more tables would be "served" in the little church. Occasionally the ministers would make what were believed to be humorous references to each other in the sermon or even in the prayer. Refreshments were to be had by the public in the whisky tent, as it was called. This was a kind of canvas booth of the ordinary fair description, where ale and rolls were sold, and strong waters too, as the name implies. The absence of John Barleycorn would have been anomalous. In the language

of Burns he was " the life o' public haunts,"—indispensable at rants, and fairs sacred and profane.

" Even godly meetings o' the saunts,
By him inspired,
When gaping they besieged the tents,
Were doubly fired."

Stools and deal benches were sometimes provided, but usually the customers stood or squatted,
each man in his own company, and refreshed
the physical man, while the spiritual appetite discussed the sermon. The stationary " public," or
" change-house," had also its quota of "yill-
caup commentators." It was filled, but and
ben, after each table. A baker from the nearest
town would have a cart-load of provisions on
the field for those who were content with solid
fare, and found their beverage in the running
burns. There was no want of waiters, who were
sometimes brought, but were oftener found in
the locality. The cottars in the neighbourhood
gave their services. There was a grand dinner
for the preachers on the following Monday at
the manse. The money collections taken at
the accesses to the tent ground defrayed the
sacramental outlay; and the balance, it was understood, purveyed the preachers' dinner. It was
calculated that as many as six thousand people
would be present at a tent preaching at Path-
Struie. The gathering was not at all of the nature
of a modern revival meeting. There was nothing

whatever in the slightest degree to warrant the comparison. It was rather the other way.

Most of the attendants at the Holy Fair, the women with scarcely an exception, brought with them, in pouch or pocket, their provisions for the day. Unless each had in this way for the most part been his own caterer, nothing short of the miraculous could have prevented the multitudes from fainting in the wilderness or by the way. They were far from the sources of supply, and even the baker's van of loaves and rolls, though supplemented by the resources of the whisky tent and the change-house, and the hospitality of the neighbouring farms, would have furnished scarcely more than a literal mouthful to the hungering thousands. Many from social forethought carried double supplies, to which the wilfully improvident trusted. However the food was come by, the festival was a veritable feast day; and in the matter of drink, if spiritual outflowings from the one tent were a feature of the gathering, spirituous libations from the other failed not before day ended to manifest in the dispersing multitudes as marked a feature. The food privately purveyed for the fair was both ampler and more luxurious than what served for ordinary occasions. It was

> " Sweet-milk cheese, in mony a whang,
> And farls, baked wi' butter,
> Fu' crump that day."

The surplus, after supplying the bearer's necessities, was large, and liberally offered where it was believed to be needed.

> " Cheese and bread, frae women's laps,
> Was dealt about in lunches,
> An' dauds that day."

Sometimes the gloaming, that usually fell so peacefully over the pastoral hills, was rudely disturbed by revellers lingering at the change-house—sons of Belial flushed with insolence and ale. The disturbance might be indicative of mirth—a snatch of a bacchanalian ballad, or a roar of choral laughter at the antics of some foolish youth advanced to the funny stage of intoxication. But it might also be the noises of wrangling and quarrelling. Disgraceful fights, not without their comic aspect, were engaged in, sides were taken, and battles ensued that involved every individual in the alehouse, till, after the demolition of much glass within, the noisier elements were bundled out of doors into the darkness, where they made such uproar as penetrated to the manse and brought out the minister to redd them. Torn coats and broken hats, to keep free of the natural covering, were the ensigns of the concluded fray ; and Tammie or Sandie, who had seemed in the rustic eye so sprucely attired in the morning, would return home at night, half defiant, half despondent, with his West-of-England frock-coat so rent in

twain, that the loose half walloped in the dust
or mud all the way behind him. The women,
they were few, who stayed till dusk, lost their
reputation. A sort of moorland shebeen, two
miles or so distant from the sacred tent, caught
a fraction of the revellers on their homeward
way, and there the revelry was renewed, and
continued into the tranquillity of midnight. It
was conducted by a certain notorious Patie,
whose hut on the heather happened to be at a
county's end. Indeed his kitchen, or but, was in
one shire, while his ben was in another, so that
it was difficult to prove locality in any charge of
illicit traffic in liquor which might be brought
against him. His was a house of call for
drouthy travellers, whatever occasion brought
them to the high Ochils. And, as a matter of
fact, a visit to Patie's, with what the visit
naturally implied, was often an end in itself. It
was believed that he smuggled, and even kept
a still. Once, his customers, a squad of geizened
weavers, drank him dry, and nearly pulled
down his house. This was at a wet holy fair
celebration, when earlier dissipation set in with
an earlier nightfall. In the fury of their
Thracian frenzy, Patie's door-lintel was borne
away bodily, his thatch scattered to the winds,
and his turf chimney-tops beaten down into the
vents. Patie himself prudently took the bent
for it, or he might have suffered the fate of

an immelodious Orpheus in the swollen Slate-
ford burn. He endured no insupportable loss.
Patie throve, and was reported to be making
"siller like sclate-stanes." Years afterwards,
when Patie's bones had been long bare in the
churchyard, the new occupant of the moorland
cottage unearthed from a nook of the kailyard
innumerable dead men, in the shape of toom
bottles and defunct jeroboams.

On a showery day the young women bound
to or from the preaching would try to save their
braws of gown and bonnet by tucking up their
dress over their heads, and hastening through
the rain to rustic scoogs or the shelter of friendly
cottages. A score of them might be found seek-
ing refuge in a roadside quarry, rough-edged
with whin, from which they would rush forth
with screams on the unexpected explosion of a
little damp gunpowder, abstracted from the discovered powder-flask of the quarryman by some
emancipated apprentice or other. A strange
sight they presented with the lining of their
gowns displayed, and an array of pouches
dangling around them like a gaberlunzie's meal-
bags. Fine weather gave fairplay to female
finery. As a rule these young countrywomen—
youth in their case, if they were single, being
generously supposed to range from fourteen to
forty—came to the rural communion becomingly
attired. Perhaps too great a fondness for the

primary colours in the adornment of their head-
gear was chargeable against them, but then this
penchant was so general that it could hardly be
viewed as evidence of vanity in the individual,
and it certainly served to brighten the too
sombre garb of their male guides and guardians.
Here and there, however, a distinct trace of un-
tutored or eccentric vanity in dress was to be
noticed among the women—such as a veil worn
open, and reaching to the by no means fairy-
like ankles of the wearer, or " buchts of ribbons,"
on each side of the head, of extravagant size,
and a conflagration of colour. With the general
love of finery went a pleasingly economical care-
fulness to preserve it, seemingly for its own sake ;
its value as a personal ornament was a secondary consideration. This trait of character would
appear to be the birthright of the fair sex. A
pretty common practice of the young women
attending the preachings must be noticed. If
the weather was dry and seasonable they would
journey barefooted, to save shoes and stockings,
and to ease their feet. Many of them at domestic
service in farmhouses went about their work on
week-days with the feet bare. At the last brook
on the journey they would pause on some inviting bank to wash the dust from their feet, and
dry them in thyme-bloom and the sun. Then
on went stockings and untarnished shoes ; then
hands were laved, perhaps faces refreshed, and

hot mouths cooled with the fragrant water; tresses and dresses were smoothed down ; and the last short stage of the journey presented sedate Sabbath looks and comely rustic figures decently attired.

Apropos of the subject of dress, reference must be made again to the precentor. The preaching was, of course, a great occasion for him. *His* place, too, was in the tent, and he had a vast host of voices to lead. There was always a figure in the tent ; when the minister sat down in the box, the precentor took his place, and filled the opening. On the day of the Holy Fair he was ennobled to a level with the minister. The pulpit became the *lettern*. His vesture was overhauled with a view to the great occasion. Probably he flourished in a new red, or figured, waistcoat, or at least in new stick-ups of phenomenal altitude and stiffness. He was lavish in the display of bosom linen ; he did not spare canvas. In nautical lingo, he crowded sail.

On the Monday morning succeeding the Holy Fair Sabbath, palefaced waifs, clad in crumpled black coats and limp linen, were to be encountered by the early shepherd, making their way home after a night's cooling in the heather. The risk of rheumatic fever had been heedlessly run to cool the whisky-distempered blood. It would take a day or two, lost to " trade," as the handicraftsman called his employment, before recovery would be made from the debauchery commenced at the Holy Fair.

What became of the tent ? It was left standing till a convenient time on the following Monday, when it was stored up for next year. It afforded a rare opportunity for diversion to any local herd who came upon it before its removal. He would summon to his side the neighbour herds, and they would go through the sacred drama burlesquing—sometimes with no little wit, and with some discriminating glimmer of the peculiarities of character—both minister and sermon. In the absence of a human audience for his improvised lecture, he would, to the entire satisfaction of his own mind, humorously address his hoofed and horned charge.

The Holy Fair had its abuses. Young people freed from the restraint of their parents, apprentices from the control of their masters, took advantage of being among promiscuous crowds of strangers, and indulged in reckless vagaries. Their best excuse they could not probably have formulated. It was to be found in the novelty of their surroundings. They were intoxicated by the beauty of the scenery, and infected by a spirit of social abandon everywhere abroad. The great want to an unregretful enjoyment of the day was plan. They had a large leisure on their hands, a commodity they had never been taught how to use, and committed themselves to the chance of the hour. Mischief, we have the authority of Dr Watts for saying, could be the only consequence. There were no Young Men's Guilds, or organisations that would bear publicity of any kind, to provide them with a rational and reputable scheme for the day. But, in spite of abuses to which it was only too liable, the Holy Fair, none will deny, was capable of doing, and did, benefit to the gathered communities in more ways than one. To toiling thousands it helped to break the deadening monotony of the year; it brought sundered communities together on a platform of holy brotherhood and religious equality; it shook into new life good old ideas that were in danger of stagnating, and furnished the mind with fresh ones; even the interchange of looks which it abundantly provided was a wholesome influence. It brought many face to face with Nature: even while they insulted, they were conscious of the gentle majesty of her maternal presence. It sank into their soul, and was an abiding influence for good.

BURNS LEAVING SCHOOL.

" My talents they were not the worst,
    Nor yet my education, O ;
Resolved was I, at least to try,
    To mend my situation, O."
                    —BURNS.

IF size were an index of age, the little
village of Kirkoswald might be taken
for one of the youngest in Scotland.
It happens, however, to be one of the very
oldest. If you count its lintels or lum-heads
you will probably set it down as including
some five or six score of households, and these,
you think, cannot have taken many twelve-
months to gather. They have taken — if
you look at the matter in this light — more
than twelve centuries! In other words, we
must go back to the middle of the seventh
century to find the commencement of the
history of that little roadside Carrick hamlet
which keeps its youth at such an advanced
age. What particular reason King Oswald
of Northumbria had in planting a Christian

Church in a secluded and boggy hollow of western Ayrshire, neither on the coast nor yet inland, it is impossible at this late date to say. His reason in a general way we know— for he was burning with all the zeal of a masterful neophyte. But round the holy edifice in that particular site grew up the clustering cottages in social community, whose representatives bear to this day the topographical name of Kirkoswald.

Its interest to the antiquary lies, of course, in its age. To the general reader its sole attraction is probably to be found in its connection with the earlier personal history of Burns, and with one of the later and most popular of his poems. For here the national bard—even then a poet, though a young one— at last brought his school-days to a close; and here in the populous old churchyard are said to rest the mortal remains of the eponymous hero of "Tam o' Shanter." Young Burns was a few months over his sixteenth year when, probably towards the end of May, and certainly — no matter what Currie and the "Encyclopædia Britannica" and Blackie have said to the contrary—in 1775, he came from his home at Mount Oliphant, south-westward some ten miles as the crow flies to the parish school of Kirkoswald to learn mensuration, surveying, and dialling—whatever that last-mentioned branch of knowledge might be.* Two considerations guided his father, old William Burnes, in making choice of the school at Kirkoswald rather than Dalrymple or Ayr, which were both in the neighbourhood, and, indeed, comparatively quite near. One was the reputation of the schoolmaster of Kirkoswald—a Mr Rodgers—for mathematical attainments, and the other the residence in Kirkoswald of Samuel Brown, the maternal uncle of the young poet, with whom he could lodge. The Browns appear to have belonged originally to Kirkoswald or the neighbourhood, and we must not forget that it was at Maybole Fair, four miles from Kirkoswald, that William Burnes first met and made the acquaintance of Agnes Brown, his future wife. It was, almost certainly, in the farm-house of the bride's father, near Kirkoswald, that the marriage took place.

* I am indebted to a correspondent of the *Scotsman* for the following note :—

"I have no doubt that the term 'dialling' simply means the use of the magnetic compass in land surveying. The compass fitted with sights which is used in mining surveying is known as a 'miner's dial,' and surveyors are still in many districts popularly spoken of as 'diallers.' The Kirkoswald course of instruction would probably also include the use of the sextant as a means of calculating distances and altitudes, so that Burns' occupation taking the sun's altitude 'in the garden one charming noon' is easily explained. I may add that similar courses of instruction were regularly given in the country parish school which I attended twenty years ago."

A village of the Kirkoswald type is conservative of its appearance and customs, and, even
allowing for the inevitable signs which mark the
lapse of years, Kirkoswald probably presents
to-day all the main, and many of the minor,
features which distinguished it a hundred and
fifteen years ago. The landscape lying around
it is certainly little altered. There is the same
close and even confining horizon, where the sky
all round rests on low arable hills, huddled
together somewhat unpicturesquely. Probably
there is more wood. The line of road is the
same. Running from Maybole on the north,
it passes between hedgerows of hawthorn, hung
here and there with bramble or boor-tree, into
the heart of the village, where it curves suddenly
onwards past the old churchyard, past the marsh
at the town end, and out into the primitive
country, with a descending sweep, and by-and-
by an open prospect towards the sea. The dip
of the road in its course of a little over two
miles from the village to the sea is between
three and four hundred feet. A lovelier walk
in summer time it would be difficult to find or
even imagine. Rough, broken banks, bushy
here, there clad with copse, are on one side ; on
the other are hedges of hawthorn, with green
braes rising above them; song-birds and singing
burns are all about, and make a continual
trebling in the ear against a fine background

of ocean bass. The shore of Ayr lies like an etching before you ; and far to the south, at the back of Girvan, are the famous hills behind which " Stinchar flows, 'mang moors and mosses many, O !" The sea is invisible at Kirkoswald, but its voice fills the street on a lown day, or when the wind is westerly. The houses are still for the most part what they were in Burns's boyhood — little whitewashed cottages with thatched roofs and heavy, hospitable lumheads, sitting in a social row by the roadside together, like cottar wives in clean mutches gossipping sedately in the sun. Each cottage has its little trimly-fenced kailyard in front or behind it, with a bed or border of the scanty plot bright with sweet-william and fragrant with apple-ringie or thyme. There want but the appearance of a black-eyed, swarthy-faced youth in one of these garden plots, and a Peggy Thomson beside him to confound his trigonometry, and the illusion would be tolerably complete. We should then have both scene and *dramatis personas*, with the re-enactment of a charming love-idyll well known to all students of the early life of Burns.

The episode here referred to, one of several which brightened the rather sombre if not quite sunless youth time of Burns, is best told in the poet's own graphic prose. The

account is given in the autobiographical letter
to Dr Moore :—

"I spent my *seventeenth*" [this is the word in the
original manuscript, and not *nineteenth*, as is commonly
supposed]—"my seventeenth summer on a smuggling
coast a good distance from home, at a noted school,
to learn mensuration, surveying, dialling" [not *drilling*,
as Blackie prints it], "*&c.*, in which I made a pretty
good progress. But I made a greater progress in the
knowledge of mankind. The contraband trade was at
that time very successful, and it sometimes happened
to me to fall in with those who carried it on. Scenes
of swaggering riot and roaring dissipation were till this
time new to me ; but I was no enemy to social life.
Here though I learned to fill my glass and to mix
without fear in a drunken squabble, yet I went on with
a high hand with my geometry, till the sun entered
Virgo, a month [August] which is [1787] always a
carnival in my bosom, when a charming fillette, who
lived next door to the school, overset my trigonometry,
and set me off at a tangent from the spheres of my
studies. I, however, struggled on with my sines and
co-sines for a few days more ; but stepping into the
garden one charming noon to take the sun's altitude,
there I met my angel

> "'Like Proserpine gathering flowers,
> Herself a fairer flower.'

It was in vain to think of doing any more good at school.
The remaining week I stayed I did nothing but craze the
faculties of my soul about her, or steal out to meet her ;
and the two last nights of my stay in the country, had
sleep been a mortal sin, the image of this modest and
innocent girl had kept me guiltless. I returned home
very considerably improved."

There are several points in this brief but comprehensive record of young Burns' experiences at Kirkoswald that we should like to dwell on. In the meantime, the history of the love adventure must suffice. The charming fillette was, of course, Peggy Thomson. She was the poet's second sweetheart. One autumn before, in 1773, he had fallen in love, for the first time in his life, with Nellie Kirkpatrick, the blacksmith's daughter, near Mount Oliphant. The expression of love with Burns required lyrical aid from the very first. He sang her praises in his earliest composition, " Handsome Nell." In 1775 he tried to sing the praises of Peggy Thomson in the song commencing— " Now breezy win's and slaughtering guns." It was his second attempt at verse, and, like the former effort, it was also meant to be sung. It was thus with song that the poetry of Burns, very characteristically, began. Everybody knows that it was with song it ended. It should also be known that he wrote more songs than non-lyrical poems. The song in praise of Kirkoswald Peggy, begun in August 1775, and of which at that time only some eight suggestive lines were got through, was completed—it runs to forty lines in all—eight years later, at a time, August or September 1783, when a renewal of his early passion for Peggy seems to have occurred. He was then living with his father at Lochlie. Little more than a year after the last-mentioned date, more particularly on 11th November 1784, he wrote from "Mossgavil" to a certain Thomas Orr, an honest rustic belonging to the neighbourhood of Kirkoswald, that he was "very glad Peggy" [for her own sake, not for his] "was off his hand, as he was embarrassed enough without her." Shortly afterwards we find Peggy married to a Mr Neilson in her native village—"my old acquaintance," said Burns of him in the Riddell MS., "and a most worthy fellow." One interview of some interest took place between Mrs Neilson and Burns in 1786. The poet describes it in the same MS.:—"Poor Peggy! . . . When I was taking leave of my Carrick relations, intending to go to the West Indies, when I took farewell of her, neither she nor I could speak a syllable. Her husband escorted me three miles on my road, and we both parted with tears." On this occasion he left with Peggy, as a parting gift and memento, a copy of his Kilmarnock Poems, with the inscription :—

" Once fondly loved, and still remember'd dear,
    Sweet early object of my youthful vows !
Accept this mark of friendship, warm, sincere—
    Friendship ! 'tis all cold duty now allows.
And when you read the simple, artless rhymes,
    One friendly sigh for him—he asks no more,—
Who distant burns in flaming torrid climes,
    Or haply lies beneath th' Atlantic's roar."

The intelligent peasantry of Scotland, and they comprise the majority of their class, have a traditional respect, that might almost be called instinctive, for knowledge and education. They have always been keenly alive to the benefits of book-learning. They have painfully sought it for themselves, in many cases with marvellous success; and they have pinched and pared to procure it for their children. It has often been the best and, indeed, the only legacy they could leave them. In sending his eldest son to Kirkoswald school, William Burnes was no doubt actuated by the laudable desire of having him equipped for the battle of life with a good general education. But he must also have had some special end in view in setting him at the age of sixteen to the study of mensuration and land-surveying with Mr Rodgers. He was probably bent on getting him fully qualified for the post of factor or land-steward, or some such situation, which, while connected with farming, should yet lift him a little above the precarious prospects of a farmer's life. How precarious those prospects generally were the old man well knew, and was yet more bitterly to know. Such a post, but of a kind, one may venture to say, which the old man neither expected nor would have desired, his son did afterwards fill. Burns's actual appointment to the duties of an excise

officer was not made till the autumn of 1789;
and the discharge of those duties, as is well
known, was found in his case to be incompatible with the business of farming. He tried
to combine the two employments for about two
years, but in 1791 he took final leave of the
farm and rural work, and removing from Ellisland to the port of Dumfries, lived for the last
five years of his life a burgess and a gauger.
There can be little doubt that his studies in
mensuration in his seventeenth summer at Kirkoswald had a direct bearing upon his future
choice of a profession, or rather upon his destiny
to the work of an exciseman.   Those duties
were a necessary part of his training for the
post ; they were the basis of his professional
preparations.   It is worthy of notice how soon
he began to turn his attention to a situation
in the excise.   It divided his mind in 1786
with the desperate scheme of emigration to
the West Indies—only it was more desirable
than attainable then.   The success of the Edinburgh edition of his poems in 1787 put it for a
while out of his head, but in the second winter
of his sojourn in Edinburgh the old idea returned, and the poet, apparently encouraged by
Clarinda, began to take active steps to have it
realised.   Its realisation seemed to the *aimless*
poet (it is his own repeated designation of himself) to be the only respectable refuge from the

fear of want or a degrading dependency. Its ultimate realisation to a man constituted as he was, and circumstanced as, for the greater part of thirty years, he had been, was ostensible ruin. It was not only that it brought him into perilous neighbourhood with the common means of conviviality, but it demanded the sacrifice of healthful rural conditions, and entailed the loss of kindly rural influences.

The few months of his residence at Kirkoswald brought Burns into contact with a new world in respect of both scenic and social surroundings. At the same time he enjoyed a freedom, hitherto unknown, to move about very much as he liked in this new world. It was his first prolonged absence from home and a rather strict paternal discipline. He was not, indeed, a total stranger to the scenery of the seaside when he came to the smuggling coast of Kirkoswald. He was not far from the sea at Alloway as a boy, and during his three weeks' stay at Ayr in 1773 he had perambulated the beach with his schoolmaster, Mr Murdoch; at Mount Oliphant, too, he had a charming glimpse of the distant sea any time he chose to lift his eyes from the furrows or the harvest-field. But at Culzean Bay, or from the low, ling-covered strand stretching southward from Turnberry Point, he probably saw for the first time, in a poetical sense, " the wan moon setting ayont the white wave." It is noteworthy, but scarcely wonderful, that Burns sings so little of the sea. The little that he has sung about it is perhaps best represented by the suggestive line just quoted. He was a true landsman. His vocation was where busy ploughs were whistlin' thrang. He had, upon the whole, a landsman's horror of the uncertain sea. There was no doubt a delight to be drawn from the dashing roar of breakers heard safely from the sounding shore ; but he shrank from a closer acquaintance with the stormy wave.

> " The whistling wind affrightens me,
> I think upon the raging sea,
> Where many a danger I must dare,
> Far from the bonnie banks of Ayr."

His horror of the sea meant an increase in his love for the land.

It was, however, the society of the locality that constituted the more novel part of young Burns's experience at Kirkoswald. The coast was as well adapted for contraband traffic in brandy and other commodities as the more notorious Solway ; and, probably, every crofter or cottar within sight of the sea for miles on both sides of Turnberry Tower smuggled if he could. Smuggling, indeed, was regarded as a praiseworthy and even patriotic breach of the law, especially by Scottish smugglers. It was not only universal, but carried on with soul, and strength, and mind; and it was, we are assured, "very successful." The inequality of the duties, it is well known, gave great encouragement to the smuggling trade between Scotland and England; it was only recently (1855) that the duties were equalised. Into this wild, nocturnal, smuggling world of adventure, and riot, and roaring dissipation young Burns was propelled, partly by accident and partly by natural temperament. The swaggering scenes rather startled him at first, but he was "no enemy to social life," and " soon learned to fill his glass and mix without fear in a drunken squabble." His sympathies were doubtless with the smugglers; he was to know them long after in a different relation on Solway side. Making due allowance for the difference of locality, one cannot be far wrong in picturing Burns in scenes in the neighbourhood of Kirkoswald in the summer nights of 1775, similar to those in which Alan Fairford is represented to have found himself in the smuggling port of Annan somewhere about the same year—as narrated in the delightful pages of " Redgauntlet." Specimens of the Tom Trumbull type on land, and of the Nanty Ewart species on sea, were doubtless to be met with on the Carrick coast, and may have been known afar off by young Burns; and his ears may have heard the clatter of hoofs and

rattling of chains in the moonlight, as the contraband kegs and barrels were conveyed on pack
saddles from the sandy downs to inland places
of concealment. He mixed, at all events, with
the smugglers in the village inn ; and if he did
not share in their adventures, he at least heard
them narrated at first hand. That a cantata of
jolly smugglers lay sleeping and unsung within
his memory, who can doubt ? Whether Douglas
Graham belonged to the fraternity of illegal
traders it is impossible to say definitely, but
that his figure and habits and history were well
known to young Burns is highly probable if he
was, as a steady tradition in the village avers,
the prototype of Tam o' Shanter. The farm of
Shanter is near Kirkoswald, and Graham's last
resting-place is in the sloping churchyard at the
south end of the village. From all that is
reported of him one may well believe that he
was at least a suggestive study for Tam. His
wife, too, would seem to have been well fitted to
enact the part of Kate—

> " Gathering her brows like gathering storm,
>   Nursing her wrath to keep it warm."

It is interesting to note, on the authority of the
stone record in the churchyard, that the tenant
of Shanter survived all the evil prophecies supposed to have been uttered in conjugal warning
for Tam's reformation, and died at the patri-
archal age of seventy-two. By the way, there

is no portrait of Tam in the poem—an omission
that is a little remarkable if Burns really did
draw from personal knowledge of Graham. That
Burns could paint a portrait is of easy proof.
He has given us the figure of Harry Erskine ;
Grose lives before us as " a fine, fat, fodgel
wight ;" Creech is " a little upright, pert, tart,
tripping wight." A well-chosen word or two,
and the individual is limned.

It was in the house of his mother's brother,
Samuel Brown, that Burns lodged during his
stay at Kirkoswald. Thirteen years afterwards
—in May 1788—he wrote to this uncle in a style
which shows how the staple trade of the village
lived in his recollection, and coloured the very
talk of the villagers. Of course this latter statement presupposes on the part of Burns a perfect
sympathy, even in language, with his correspondent—a sympathy which the letters of Burns,
taken altogether, undoubtedly reveal. At the
date of this particular letter the poet was on the
eve of his marriage with Jean Armour, and was
making preparations for furnishing their future
home at Ellisland.

"Dear Uncle," he writes, "this I hope will find you
and your conjugal yoke-fellow in your good old way. I am
impatient to know if the Ailsa fowling be commenced for
this season yet, as I want three or four stones of feathers,
and I hope you will bespeak them for me. It would be a
vain attempt for me to enumerate the various transac-
tions I have been engaged in since I saw you last ; but

this know—I engaged in a smuggling trade, and no poor man ever experienced better returns, etc." [He refers allegorically to his private marriage, which the Church, represented at Mauchline by Daddy Auld, refused to sanction; and goes on to intimate that he means to be a fair-trader in future.] "I have taken a farm on the banks of Nith, and in imitation of the old patriarchs, get men-servants and maid-servants, and flocks and herds, and beget sons and daughters.—Your obedient nephew, ROBERT BURNS."

We have Samuel Brown's disposition reflected in this letter. Like his sister, the poet's mother, he was apparently frank, easy-going, humorous, and contented. The contrast to old William Burnes is well-nigh perfect. Samuel Brown is addressed as "dear uncle;" his own father is "honoured sir." In his uncle's house Burns enjoyed a latitude of speech and behaviour to which he had been a stranger. Mrs Brown seems to have been a worthy helpmeet to her husband. She had no children of her own, but assisted in her function as *howdie* in bringing many children into the world. So, at least, reports William Marshall, the aged occupant of a farm in Canada, who, if we are not misinformed, has occupied in his youth the same saddle with Luckie Brown in several moonlight, midnight scampers on hasty summons to the house of birth.

Burns returned home from Kirkoswald to Mount Oliphant, as he says, "very considerably improved." Previous to this visit he had

been "perhaps the most ungainly awkward
boy in the parish," and as unacquainted with
the ways of the world as a hermit. The parish
he refers to was the united parishes of Alloway
and Ayr—not, as so many editors copying
each other state, the parish of Tarbolton. In
the original MS. of the autobiographical letter
to Dr Moore it is distinctly written that the
summer spent on the smuggling coast was his
seventeenth. Dr Currie, in 1800, misquoted the
passage so as to read nineteenth, and subsequent editors went on repeating the error till
the correction was made by, we think, the late
Mr Scott Douglas. On his return to the farm
Burns mixed more freely in the rather scattered
society of his neighbourhood, and to give his
manners a brush—as he phrased it—began to
attend a country dancing school, in conscious
opposition to his father's wishes. This school
was probably at Dalrymple. Unfortunately for
both father and son, this act of disobedience on
the part of young Burns produced an estrange-
ment which was never afterwards removed.
William Burnes was not, at least in theory, the
strict and strait-laced Calvinist that many believed him to have been. The Catechism of
religious belief which Murdoch wrote to his
dictation is proof of this. But he was "irascible
and subject to strong passions," and was not
likely to forgive in his eldest son any disregard

of his will, even though the natural instinct of
youth for social recreation should prompt it.
The iniquity of promiscuous dancing may have
been bad enough in the eyes of the elder Burns,
but the deliberate disobedience of a son was
worse ; it was unpardonable.   It was a miserable enough matter to differ about, but in its
results it was scarcely less than tragic to both.
With the forfeiture of his father's esteem, young
Burns became regardless and dissipated ; his
disobedience and dissipation were thorns in
the pillow of his father, which the old man,
as he lay on his death-bed, may have thought
were of his own placing.   He might so reason-
ably have granted the permission.   In a short
time the young poet lost all his awkwardness
of demeanour, became self-possessed, bold, and
easy of address, and was the acknowledged
king of every rustic gathering.

THE REVOLUTION IN THE RURAL DISTRICTS.

IT is difficult, if not impossible, for a son of the city to realise the changes that have taken place during the last half-century or so among the inhabitants of our remoter rural districts. These changes, indeed, have been so great as to amount in many localities to a revolution. Whole tracts of country, even in the lowlands south of the Tay, have become either absolutely depopulated, or their occupants have been thinned to the merest fraction of their former numbers. With the people have, of course, disappeared a great number and a great variety of rural industries. In at least one aspect of it, the revolution is a sad one. Where before were social hamlets and hospitable homesteads, bright with a busy and contented population, mostly dependent on each other for livelihood and happiness, are now empty houses and dilapidated steadings, with an occasional vagrant temporarily disputing their possession with the wind and rain. In sunshine, even the homeless beggar keeps aloof from them. The fields in the neighbourhood are unenlivened by human presence ; the wheel-tracks are choked with grass, and the footpaths are only distinguishable at a distance. It does not, of course, follow that the former inhabitants of those vacant areas have been lost to the nation. They have been lost to what is known (the phrase being used in a a restricted sense) as *the country*—the open rural parts of the kingdom. There has simply been a redistribution of the rural population, with a marked determination of the movement to the greater centres of commerce and manufacture. It would be wrong, on the general question of this migration of country folks to towns, to write it down as the enforced result of tyrannical landlordism. Neither landlord greed nor tenant greed was the prime or main cause of it. It has rather been the voluntary movement of the country enticed into the town by the offer, or in hope, of higher wages and richer prospects. And if compulsion has been felt, and the exchange of green lanes and open roadsides for close confining streets and the sombre air of cities has been reluctantly made, it is a compulsion as natural and inevitable as the rise of the tide. The pressure has been caused by the developments of science in the industrial world, and the altered conditions of industrial life which these developments imply. The exchange, too, has not been by any means universally regretted. Regrets there have been, and are—chiefly expressed by those who were too advanced in life, or too conservative of their old habits, to yield to the pressure which urged the exchange, or who yielded and were disappointed in their dreams of the town.

There are none but poetical regrets from those that have prospered by the exchange. These poetical regrets are few ; the class from which they come is large. But it is not all gain even with the successful majority. There is a loss which they may easily overlook. There is danger that the virtues which bloomed in the country may fade in the town. There is fear that in many transferred households they do. The loss of the rural virtues is unfortunately not incompatible with the increase of material comforts and even intellectual advantages. It was not simply the loss of so many peasants to the Village of the Plain—there went with them contentment, and hospitality, and connubial tenderness, and

"Piety with wishes placed above,
And steady loyalty, and faithful love."

These, in the poet's view of the movement, already commencing in his day, were the price-less exports that went in the emigrant ship. There is a danger almost as great, that the practice of these virtues is weakened or abandoned by simple migration from the country to the town. The other day I stopped on the high-road to chat with a stone-breaker who was smoking beside his bing. A deserted and utterly decayed farm-town of the smaller class was in view. "Very few folk," he said, "ken the name o' that auld toon. But I was a laddie there fifty years syne, livin' wi' my faither. That's Buchtleys. It's pairt o' a big farm, an' has nae name noo. My faither had a pair o' horses an' sax kye, forby sheep, on that bit place; and in that hoose my fowre sisters were trained to service by their mither. I wonder whare the gentry get their hoose servants noo. For mysel', I was a kin' o' wastrel; tried Glesca; ran aff to America; an' here I am, knappin' stanes within sicht o' my faither's hoose. It was a couthier hame than I've kent since I left it: at least it was a happier. An' Scotland was a heartier kintra to live in." He put his pipe in his pocket, and rose up. "I mind when there was a tenant in a' thae toom hooses yont the road. An' the road gaed just like a street in a thrivin' toun—noo a carriage, an' noo a gig,

folk on fit, wi' here an' there a man i' the
saiddle; then there were lang strings o' cairts
for coals, or wi' claith frae the bleach - field,
forby carriers an' cadgers; an', of coorse, the
coaches, as reg'lar's the clock, baith mornin'
an' nicht. Ye were never oot o' sicht o' some-
body; ye needit na to be weary. Noo a' thae
residenters are soopit into toons, or aff the flure
o' Scotland a'thegither; an' baith traivellin' an'
traffic ha'e ta'en to the railroad. Man, ye're
the third body that has past me this day, an'
the first that hailed me; an' for traffic—a
herrin' cairt drave by aboot twal o'clock! I've
sma' use o' my tongue on this road, an' there's
hardly mair for a knappin'-hammer!" He
lifted the tool as he named it, and seemed
about to resume his work. But first he went
on—"The muckle - farm system did a' the
mischief; an' the lairds are noo findin' oot
that mischief it was. Na, na! the kintra
pairt o' Scotland 'll no' be richt till the sile 's
paircell'd oot maybe sma'er than afore, an'
folk entised back to 't frae the touns. An'
the suner the better, for the langer the waur!"

This was the testimony of the roadside,
uttered by a regretful representative. In old
Gibbie Doss I found a resigned representative
of the stranded village. A strange pride
mingled with his resignation, which was perhaps the pride of the historian. "There's little

o' a toun left," said Gibbie, "either in hoose or
inhabitant. I dinna think there's owre three
looms gaun, tho' there's thretty or mair thrang
rottin' i' the auld factories. It's forty years
sin' there was an apprentice, an' the lad was at
the treddles only a few years. He's a roadman
noo, an' disna ken a shuttle frae a shoe-horn, a'
warrand. There's naebody here but auld folk,
an' single folk; and there's naebody to tak'
their place when they gang. The young folk
a' leave—there's naething to keep them. Jist
begin at the wall (*well*) alang there, an' come
doun the toun. Weel, there's Tam Roy an' his
wife—his folk are a' grown up, an' awa'. Then
there's Kirsty Doo—there's nae howp o' her.
Willie Mill comes next; he's no' often here;
comes back frae his toun frien's for a week or
twa i' the spring to plant his yaird an' sweir at
my hens; he canna get onybody to buy his
hoose. Weel, the next hoose to him is emp'y.
Its neibor across the wey wants baith a ruif an'
a tenant. Wha's next? Peter Anderson—a
povy body as ony i' the parish; but he has nae
bairns, tho' he's been thrice marriet. There's
the bellman next door; his family are a' awa'
but ane, a lamiter. Then there's Nell Aither
an' her cat; an' Willie Black—he keeps a soo.
The precentor's opposite; he's a stranger, wi'
nae family but a noospaper chop. An' here
am I; my folk widna bide at hame; there was

naething to keep them. I expect Mag the morn on a veesit. An' that's the gate o't, gang this way or that thro' the haill toun. There hasna a hoose been biggit for a score o' years. The auld slater has nae wark but the soopin' o' lums. John Rissle ran awa' fra his hoose an' his fowre-acre field; he couldna get a rent for them, that wad pay their feu to the laird!"

The effects of the revolution that has desolated the social and industrial life of the remoter rural districts of Scotland since the commencement of the century, cannot, perhaps, be more vividly realised than by a study of the annals of some particular hamlet or hill-side that has suffered from the change. These are mostly unwritten annals, to be gathered only from the memories of aged men, whose youth was familiar with the ways of the older world. Of these aged historians, the loudest and liveliest are not, as might, perhaps, be imagined, the few original residenters who have survived the mutations which have been gradually desolating their neighbourhood, but returned emigrants, whether from the colonies or from the big towns at home, to whom the interval of their absence, like an abolition of the years, brings into eloquent contrast the difference between past and present. To them the condition of their native village and district, as it showed in their youth, is like a thing of yesterday. To-day it has vanished, and, with the bewilderment of Mirza, they gaze on a change of scene.

We propose to take a glance at that old social and industrial life as it was exemplified in an Ochil valley. The sun shone upon this valley in the early part of the present century, to see it pulsating with a varied and contented activity: it now shines upon a comparative solitude. The number of its former occupants is reduced to a handful; several of its homesteads are merely names which hover around the traces of human habitation faintly seen on the hill-side; other homesteads are scenes of uninhabitable decay, silent and smokeless, and open to the elements; some of its industries have ceased to be practised, while others have been arrested almost to the point of stagnation; and social neighbourhood is almost impossible, from the long intervals which sunder family from family. The weekly meeting at the little church is almost the only means of union to most of its scanty inhabitants. Their personal intercourse with the outer world is by attendance at a market once or twice a year. The outer world comes to them once a week or so in the shape of a newspaper, or a grocer's spring-cart, or a baker's van.

The valley referred to—that of the Water of

May, and more especially the upper half of it—
presents no extreme case of the neglect which
has overtaken many of our rural districts. It
is a fairly representative instance.

The rich and romantic scenery of a small
portion of its lower course has had the happy
accident of a poetical notice, which has carried
the name of the stream further than its mere
size would warrant—for its length, from the
rushy bed on the hill-side, where it rises, to
its junction with the Earn beneath the famous
Birks, is perhaps not more than ten or twelve
miles. Half-way down its valley, on a high
green bank which slopes suddenly to the
romantic haugh formed by its union with the
Chapel-burn, is perched in an open atmosphere,
and yet snugly sheltered by hills, the decayed
but still picturesque hamlet of Path-Struie. In
former years it was the centre of the social
life which throbbed through the valley. The
meeting-house was there—the inhabitants were
mostly Dissenters; the school was there; the
public-house was not far off; the shops were
there. Thither at evening came the outdoor
labourers of the neighbourhood to solace their
wearied bodies with a snuff and a dram, and to
forget their private cares in the discussion of
the cares of the community, or even those of
the nation. There is not a loom in the village,
or a weaver in the neighbourhood, now; lint is

an unknown crop ; the public-house is only a
recollection ; the little meal-mill has long since
ceased to hum ; and if there are superior school
accommodation and appliances, and a church
whose various agencies are vigorously adminis-
tered, neither the scholars nor the worshippers
are anything like so numerous as they used to be.

Between the head of the May and the vicinity
of the village, a distance from west to east of
five or six miles, the population of the water-
side was collected into such knots, in farms and
pendicles, as were represented by the following
names. Even the names of human habitations
in country places are not without interest ; they
smack of rurality, and are usually expressive of
the physical or legendary features of the localities
which they distinguish. There were The Corb-
Glen, Midge - mill, Craig - baiky, Lead - green,
Knowe - head, Reshie - hill, Boads - head, Bank-
head, White-fields, Rouchle-slap, Clow, Cooper's-
hill, Wauk-mill, Struie-mill, West-side, Mount-
hoolie, Path-green, Path-mill, Path-foot, The
Syke, Condie, and a few others. Some of these
are now nothing but names, and probably not
one of them maintains a dependency equal in
number to that with which it was once enlivened. It has neither the interest nor the
dignity with which a far more numerous dependency of human beings formerly invested it
The valley is mostly in grass; old rigs have grown,

E

strange to the plough ; walls have been levelled; trees cut; foundations razed. The shepherd has almost entirely superseded the ploughman, and the larger farm has devoured the smaller. With the plough and the pendicle have largely disappeared handicrafts and cottar industries.

On the very ridge of Cooper's-hill there was, sixty years ago, a large piece of common land, or "commonty," on which, free of all expense, except the penny fee of the herd, the cottars around Path-Struie grazed their cows. In occasional years even the slender charge of the herd was saved, and the kye would come home from pasture at the sound of a horn. The farmers were not above imitation of the cottars in utilising the common. The bounds of the common were never clearly defined. Old men held that it was a disused drove-road, and ran perhaps all the way over the Ochils to Auchterarder. It was four hundred yards broad, or so, and was allowed to be miles in length. In clear September weather the view from the common on Cooper's-hill was absolutely grand ; it was exhilarating. The commanding domes of the solidly-built Lomonds were in view on one side; in the far north were the snowy Grampians, a visible proof to the juvenility of the village that the world was large. It was entirely an inland view ; the hills at the back of Ardargie (known to the Romans), and of Rossie-Ochil to the north-east, shut out the questing sea. The common no longer exists. It has been gradually and silently enclosed—appropriated, in the first instance, as the most effectual means, by the plough, and then thrown into pasture, which reveals in its rigs the marks of ownership. Its present ownership is possibly best known to the neighbouring lairds.

The May, and its tributary, the Chapel—which, running parallel with it, is at no part of its course more distant from the larger stream than about two miles—are good trouting burns, and at one time, before the interference of game-keepers, were much frequented by anglers. They would come all the way from Perth to fish the May, which had the larger pools, and promised heavier trout. The anglers were chiefly shop-keepers, with a sprinkling of professional men, and now and then a few of the gentry. The local farmers never fished — it was too paltry an occupation, and too childish a pastime for their honest prejudices. As for shepherds, with a large leisure on their hands, and rare opportunities for piscatorial knowledge — they were too lazy. Donald, to use the class name of the northern shepherds, was a gentleman in this respect, that he never "cuist his coat" to work. You might see him do that reverence to the sun on a particularly hot day in August, as he sweltered slowly along a glowing hill side with his jacket sleeves depending helplessly

from his left arm, and Oscar responding to his
pants behind him. He had a clearly defined
idea of his duties to his employer—which was
to tend the sheep only. He considered himself
a cut above a low-country shepherd, who has,
when the season demands it, to take hoe in hand
at the head of women workers in the turnip
field — whose shepherding, indeed, is for the
most part confined to a visit to the flock at
morn, and again at even, with farm work waiting
for him in the long interval between. But the
Highland shepherds of the Ochils—nearly all
clansmen in the early part of the century—
Maclarens, Macdonalds, Macdiarmids, Mackillie-
wees, Menzieses, and Gows—claimed the time
which did not require active pastoral work as
their own ; and employed it, not in angling, but
in various industries which we usually regard as
domestic. Donald mended his own shoes. He
carried needle and thread in his bonnet, and
repaired his breeches, on the hill side if necessary, in journeymanlike style. And when there
was nothing else to do, he produced the wires,
and, from a clew of worsted in his pocket,
knitted stockings and mittens for the winter.
The thread, of course, was homespun. Neither
did he work just for his own comfort in the
matter of personal clothing. He knitted for
anybody who would engage his services. But
shepherds, when the valley was in its most

populous and prosperous state, were comparatively few. They began to increase after the
first quarter of the century, and the new-comers
were not always generally welcome. The feeling of the rural community on the advent of
Donald was expressed at the time by a local
bard, David Smith by name, whose verse, by
the way, though not without certain Blake-like
touches in its appreciation of the loveliness of
life, especially the life of children, is chiefly of
value as a record in writing—the only one we
know of—of the deserted valley of the May.
David's prophetic sentiments in 1835 were
these—

> " If herdsmen and shepherds must only be seen
> Where numerous and thriving the people have been,
> They'll get on the fingers, they'll suffer, I trow,
> Who basely discourage the harrow and plough."

The contingency feared became a fact;

> " Since now the dull shepherd is all that can be,
> Where fine stirring village was lightsome to see."

Spinning was an occupation formerly practised under every roof in the valley. Weaving,
too, was a common employment. There were
"customer" weavers, as they were called, who
made cloth for the consumer,—the local farmers,
and others. Their customers supplied the yarn;
and in some solitary, but not unsocial, hut on
the hill slope, the textile fabric bargained for

was duly produced from the little manufactory of a single loom. The whir of the flying shuttle, and the beat of the "lay" as it closed up the woof into the web, were familiar sounds to the denizens of the valley. The herd-boy heard them where he loitered in the bracken beside his charge on the sunny brae; and they cheered the gloom for the belated ploughman, returning from the smithy with irons dressed for to-morrow's darg. The customer weavers were generally reported, rightly or wrongly, to be "awfu' deevils for stealin' yairn." Willie Wastle of Linkum-doddie, the reader may remember, was "a wabster guid," and, on Burns's authority, he had the wabster's weakness for thread—he "could stow a clew wi' onybody." The weakness was as incidental to the craft as cabbaging to tailors, and of course it was made ministrant to a similar end. There was another class of weavers, who worked for the manufacturers of the large towns. This class resided chiefly in the village, and wove in their own houses. But there was at least one four-loomed shop in the village, the clacking of which, when the whole four machines were going, gave quite a town air to the little community. Cotton, perhaps, was the staple manufacture for the foreign trade of the village: its textile products for the home market were linen and woollen goods. The weavers, as being tradesmen, were rather de-

spised by the farmers, who have still an ill-
deserved and misapplied contempt for all
sedentary craftsmen. " Gae 'wa', laddie!" a
farmer would say to a youth, whom he had
recently fee'd for agricultural work, "you'll
never be worth saut to your kail aboot a ferm ;
be a wabster!" The weavers on the Water of
May were not pale, and meagre, and "shilpit,"
like town weavers; but the confinement and
light exercise gave them a somewhat spare
habit of body. They were a healthy enough
class of men, though they did not present the
sunburnt robustness of ploughmen. They were
not the pallid, undersized weavers whom George
Eliot found in Raveloe. They were thinkers,
who discussed religion at the fireside, and
politics at the alehouse. Some of them were
poachers, most of them sang—sentimental songs
were favoured—and all of them had a store of
anecdotes for the entertainment of a customer,
or a guest. Not one of them would have
answered to the type Shakespeare furnishes in
Bottom, though the name is universally applic-
able, and has been chosen with the eye of an
artist; but several of them met Falstaff's infer-
ential description of the craft: "I would I were
a weaver,—I could sing psalms or anything."

A hundred years ago the farmers' contempt
for weavers did not exist. Weaving was then a
lucrative business, and even bonnet lairds of

some standing made their sons weavers. There
is a well-authenticated story of a bonnet laird,
who had his son educated in the mysteries of
weaving, and built him a shop on the roadside
on the outskirt of his land, that his industry
might be commanded from the farm-house.
The lighted "creuzie" in the shop of a winter
evening was evidence to the parents that Robbie
was assiduous at his toil. "Yonder's Robbie's
lamp," they said to each other, and were
satisfied. Meanwhile the lamp shone upon an
idle loom, and young Hopeful, as likely as not,
was in the adjacent burrowstoun, drinking and
delighting himself with his boon companions.
With the destruction of the small farms began
the contempt for weaving. Farmers, for a
dozen years or so before 1848, supplied the
markets with corn very much at their own
price, made money fast, and grew uppish.
Then came the repeal of the Corn Laws. But
there was still the protection of the cost of
carriage upon imported grain (from America),
of about half-a-guinea on the quarter. The half-
guinea has fallen to eighteenpence, and, owing
to swift steamers and the great development of
supply from abroad, may fall to the half of that.

In the days of small farms, fifty acres—
thirty for crop and the remainder for needful
pasture—gave employment to a pair of horses.
It did not pay to keep a pair on less than fifty

acres, so divided, unless the small farmer hired out his horses to "labour" a neighbour's croft. It was no uncommon thing to run six small farms into one large one, with the result that a great proportion of the rural inhabitants were thrown out of their former way of living, and betook themselves to the towns in search of a livelihood.

Mills for grain and lint were a notable feature in the industrial life of the valley in the earlier part of the century. They were small, but numerous, and gave employment to many families. A small farm was usually attached to each mill. There were as many as nine oatmeal and barley mills on the May, all "customer" mills, with the benefit of thirlage. These were—Midge Mill, Clow Mill, Path Mill, Struie Mill (it was here that David Smith, the afore-mentioned rhymer, was born, and lived, and kept—"in the heart of a hill," as he says— the first Sabbath school, perhaps, in the Ochils ; it was a mill before the Restoration, " but now not a vestige appears to the eye " ; David states its age in a style of his own :

> " Put down sixteen hundred, and then fifty-six,
> And this as its date to the mill I affix.")

To continue the list : there were Condie Mill, Benzion (pronounced Bingen) Mill—which was also a lint mill—Muckersie Mill, Mill o' May, and Forteviot Mill. There is probably only one of these mills going to-day.

Flax was a pretty common crop in those days. A small field of it in blossom, with its delicate fairy-blue bells bending in the wind, gave an additional charm to the valley landscape. The crop required considerable attention in the field before it got to the mill. It was rippled to take off the "bows" (bolls), which yielded oil, etc. The rippling comb was used in the field where the flax had been pulled up. There were so many workers rippling, and so many pulling. The rippled stalks were then bound into sheaves, and put into a dam to rot the inside tissue. Large stones laid upon them kept the sheaves under water. The skin of the stalk was the valuable part of the plant. It was green when it went into the dam—white when it came out. By-and-by the water was run off, and the bundles forked out, and spread on the lea to dry after their month's steeping. They were next sent to the mill, where they were beaten free of the rotted stalk. What remained after this process was tied up, and sent off to the town to the hecklers.

Part of a ploughman's fee was usually a "lippie's bounds o' lint." That meant that about a quarter of a peck of lint-seed was sown for him. His wife spun the lint, and the weaver made sheets or cloth for his shirts out of it. The ploughman's "sark" might thus be sown, grown, woven, and worn on the farm where he worked. There was at first great antipathy to cotton cloth among the peasantry: it was believed to be unhealthy.

The capture of steam in the toils of machinery has made all the difference between past and present. To it is ultimately traceable the revolution which has been wrought in the rural districts. The shrewd eye of old David Smith, though it did not carry him far into the future, detected it as the cause of the changes he so sincerely lamented. He denounced it, though not for Mr Ruskin's reason, with a heartiness that would refresh Mr Ruskin's soul. " *That* steam," he says, with quite a classical use of the demonstrative—

> " That steam is a pow'r that's invented to serve
> Where legions unheeded are likely to sterve."

But he was averse to the innovation of mechanical means of all kinds, other than those which long use and wont had consecrated to social and domestic life. Hear his ironical strains : poverty is reigning in the but and the ben, and the poor are being crushed ;

> " The horses, however, may laugh and grow fat,
> For ease and abundance—they've plenty of that ;
> The horses may sing, and of pleasure partake—
> *The threshing is done by a stream from the lake!* "

The hum of the meal-mill is silenced at Path-Struie ; the clack of the hand-loom is heard no longer ; the cow-horn is mute for ever ; " peeble

Johnny's" hammer resounds no more in the agate quarry; the carrier, Tammy Wanton, and his white aiver, Jolly, have long since disappeared from the vista, and are without successors. There are sheep where there was corn, and turnips where there was lint; there are roofless homesteads where there were happy families; there is silence where there were the cheerful sounds of rural labour. From the lairds and farmers that remain the old style has vanished. *This* was the old style, as David Smith has testified :—

" To kirk and to market with spouse they would ride,
  Well-mounted and harnish'd in old Scottish pride ;
  Their saddles were sackcloth, embolster'd with straw,
  Their bonnets and wigs gat them rev'rence and awe ;
  Their boots were grey-mashes, their spur was a wand,
  Nor cared they for stirrup on which they might stand.
  What wives they selected to sweeten their life
  Were never called mistress, but only guidwife ;
  On Sabbaths, or when they a distance would go,
  Their hoods were jet-black, over mutches of snow ;
  Their smocks were of harn, for weel they could spin,
  And aye they were warm and clean at the skin ;
  Their church-going gown—it was damask with flow'rs,
  More costly than aught in this age that is ours ;
  And lastly a scarlet, or coal-riddle plaid ;
  Then, then they would think themselves rightly array'd."

The Ochil lairds and their spouses are conservative of many an old custom, but it must be confessed they have changed a great deal of all this.

BURNS INTRODUCING HIMSELF.

"I come to claim the common Scottish name with you, my illustrious countrymen ; and to tell the world that I glory in the title."—*Dedication to the First Edinburgh Edition of his* POEMS.

THERE was no formal reception of the new *Makkar* who had come fresh from the November furrows to Edinburgh, and now stood on the pavement

"with his ploughman stoop,
And his black flaming eyes."

There had been but a side invitation, suggested rather than expressed—the invitation of Dr Blacklock, conveyed to Burns from the manse of Loudon, and after some delay, by the hands of Gavin Hamilton. The invitation, slender though it was, probably jumped with the bard's intention of reconnoitring the capital with a view to the publication of a new edition of his poems. There was, no doubt, in the proud

heart of the poet a little chagrin at the refusal
of Wee Johnnie to undertake a second edition
without such ample guarantee against loss as
had made the first venture safe. Another list
of local subscribers was not to be—perhaps
was never even—thought of; the poet was too
poor to advance the cost of the paper ; and the
canny printer at Killie was too cautious to go
farther than he could see. It is allowed that
he had weak eyes, which were open only to
narrow interests. But the poet's ambition was
not to be snuffed out by the parsimony of a
provincial publisher. There was a world elsewhere to which he would appeal. He was then
as certain of his possession of unusual power
as he was at any time afterwards to be. The
confirmation of subsequent popular applause
raised in no degree the estimate which from
the first he had formed of his poetical ability.
The "rustic bard" accordingly stalked into
Edinburgh one day in the end of November.
The historical memories of the place took a
firm hold of his imagination at once. The
romantic site of the old city had doubtless its
effect; but mere scenic loveliness, severed from
human associations, had comparatively small
interest for Burns. It was the Castle rather
than the rock which rears it so picturesquely
to the sky; it was the forsaken seat of "Legis-
lation's sovereign powers" rather than the

ridge of hill upon which it rests; it was ancient
Holyrood rather than the beetling crags and
green slopes of Arthur's Seat, in whose shadow
it lies, that chiefly caught and kept his eye,
and thrilled with mingled awe and tenderness
the romantic chords of his heart. It is, of
course, not denied that he was an enthusiastic
admirer of the natural scenery in and around
Edinburgh. His walks and talks in the neighbourhood—with Naysmith, the artist, on many
a morning, to Arthur's Seat, to see the sun rise
from the sea, and with Dugald Stewart to the
Braids and towards the Pentlands—sufficiently
prove that he was. But even the natural landscape, however lovely, acquired its chief charm
in his view from its connection with rural
labour and rustic life; the sight of smoking
cottages gave him more pleasure than the
Arcadian scenery in the midst of which they
were set.

Life in the historical city contrasted sharply
with the life from which he had just emerged.
Robust though he was, both of body and mind,
the contrast was powerful enough, in its action
upon a nature of extreme sensitiveness, to affect
his physical well-being, and throw him, as we
say, " out of sorts " for several weeks. He had
constant headaches for more than a fortnight
after his arrival. To the inhabitants he remained "in his auld use and wont." He entered

their fashionable and literary circles, in no ways overawed either by the titles of rank or the reputation of learning. But neither did he despise the distinctions of society. There was no formal introduction, as there had been no formal invitation. If Blacklock's letter brought him to Edinburgh, it was not upon Blacklock that he waited immediately on his arrival. Probably Dugald Stewart, and the friends of Dalrymple of Orangefield, were the first persons to whom he presented himself. In a few days he had made acquaintance with rank and fashion, as represented by the Duchess of Gordon and the Glencairn family; and with law and learning, as represented by Henry Erskine and the professorial brethren of Dugald Stewart. Henry Mackenzie, who then represented literature, was also his friend, and announced in the *Lounger* to the literary world beyond Edinburgh the rare merits of the new poet. Burns may be said to have formally introduced himself to Edinburgh when Creech had his poems ready for sale. With these poems in his hand he made his ceremonious bow, and introduced himself to the notice of literary Edinburgh. What he said on the occasion is contained in his prose " Dedication," and in his better known poetical " Address." But this was not the first time that, hat in hand, so to say, Burns stood behind the footlights. There was a previous appear-

ance about nine months before; only—to keep
up the metaphor—it was in a provincial theatre,
and the audience consisted for the most part of
men with whose ways he was intimately familiar;
for they were very much his own.   The preface
to the Kilmarnock Edition of his poems is the
worst specimen of Burns's prose that we know.
It was probably written in haste.   It is ungram-
matical, tautological, pedantic, inconsistent.   Yet
it gives the impression of a man of a vigorous
mind, capable in a rough and ready fashion of
making his mark anywhere, and in other ways
than with the pen.   There is a robust personality
in it, which comes forward now and again in the
latter half, with the clearness of genuine sincerity, from amidst a mist of appropriated
phrases.   It is the idea of supercilious criticism
that rouses him to the expression of natural
feeling.   For example: "If any critic catches
at the word 'genius,' the author tells him,
once for all, that he certainly looks upon
himself as possessed of some."   And, "If I
stand fairly convicted of dulness and nonsense,
let me be done by as I would do by others
—let me be condemned without mercy to
contempt and oblivion."   There is something here which makes his application of
the word "trifles" to his poems either in-
sincere or at least conventional.   Some phrases

F

are happy and characteristic, and show the
ambition of a master of style; such are
"The glorious dawnings of poor, unfortunate
Fergusson," "My highest pulse of vanity,"
and "Kindling at the flame of the elder
poets."

The Dedication to the Caledonian Hunt of
the first Edinburgh Edition, written on the 4th
April 1787, is a most remarkable production.
It is poetical in its imagery, its bold (and just)
assumptions, and its outspoken fearlessness.
The modern taste is offended with the big
initial letters, which are meant to emphasise
the rhetoric, and with the frequent personifica-
tion of abstract qualities and conditions; but
there is genuine feeling under these rhetorical
encumbrances. The style is no mere stand of
armour; there is a warrior under the mail, and
fearless eyes flash through the barred helmet.
The characteristic touches here are such as—
"Where should I so properly look for patronage
as to the illustrious of my native land?" "The
poetic genius of my country found me like
Elisha at the plough, and threw her inspiring
mantle over me." "I do not present this Address with the venal soul of a servile author;
I was bred to the plough, and am independent."
This reveals the kind of patronage he looked
for. Again, "I come to claim the common
Scottish name with you, my illustrious country-

men." But it also contains a prayer! "I come to proffer my warmest wishes to the Monarch of the Universe for your welfare and happiness." A noticeable feature is the unenvious, the noble sympathy of this ploughman with the noblemen and gentlemen of the Hunt both in their social pastime and in the privacy of their domestic happiness :—"When you go forth to waken the echoes in the ancient and favourite amusement of your forefathers, may Pleasure ever be of your party; and may Social joy await your return! When harassed in courts or camps with the jostlings of bad men and bad measures, may the honest consciousness of Worth attend your return to your native Seats, and domestic Happiness with a smiling welcome meet you at your gates!" Was ever a band of noblemen addressed in such fashion by a ploughman before? There is a passage in the Dedication —penned, it may be noticed in passing, doubtless at a sitting; for the strain, though elevated, is connected, and quite sustained from commencement to close — which one cannot read without recalling the metrical "Address to Edinburgh," so much and so mysteriously maligned by the late Alexander Smith. "While tuning my wild artless notes to the rural loves and joys of my native Kyle," says the poet in effect in his Dedication, and almost in these words, "the genius whispered me to come to this ancient metropolis, and lay my songs before you." The same image, softened and beauti-fied, and expressed with a charming modesty, appears in the Address—

" From marking wildly-scatter'd flowers,
    As on the banks of Ayr I stray'd,
And singing, lone, the lingering hours,
    I shelter in thy honour'd shade."

The old associations of Edinburgh had an overpowering effect upon his imagination which chastened his spirit and softened his self-asser-tion. The gentlemen of the Caledonian Hunt produced no such effect. He approached them with a demand—it is too regal to be called a request—for their patronage, and gave them, with the unconscious carelessness of a genuinely incidental allusion, an interpretation of patron-age which deprived them of flattery if they looked for it. He claims common ground with them as a loyal Scotsman, whose highest ambi-tion was to sing in his country's service; and without concealing his rank and garb, accosts them with the frankness of an equal and the affection of a brother. Burns introduced him-self without reserve. It was his way, and the nobleness of it none can deny. It would probably have been better for his material welfare if he had exercised a little reserve, and submitted to his patrons with more docility

on the one hand, and less emphatic demonstra-
tion of gratitude on the other.   Neither in
accepting favours nor in receiving advice was
he the model protégé that Patronage loves to
take in hand.

THE OLD SCOTTISH PLOUGHMAN.

" To plough and sow, to reap and mow,
My father bred me early, O ;
For one, he said, to labour bred,
Was a match for Fortune fairly, O."
—BURNS.

OF all industries those of the field are the oldest, the most widespread, and the most largely followed. Yet in respect of the condition of the workers and the methods they employ, rural toil until within recent years has undergone comparatively little change. Even in Scotland, which is generally regarded as the home of scientific farming, the primitive spade is still an implement of husbandry in the cultivation of the croft ; and in remote farms in the far north the wooden plough drawn by oxen may yet be seen breaking the soil. The sickle is not yet quite superseded, the sound of the flail still echoes in upland barns, and even the hand-mill is in occasional use in huts of the Hebrides. Piers Ploughman — gaunt, rude, ignorant, coarsely fed, roughly clad, wretchedly housed—is still a figure in the farm landscape. The condition of our tillers of the ground and their industrial methods have, however, undergone great changes for the better during the last fifty years ; and the nation has profited by the improvements. The soil has been made greatly more productive ; the use of machinery has economised both labour and produce ; the peasantry are more intelligent, have a larger share of material comfort, and are in a condition for the development of freer enterprise or the exercise of a manlier contentment.

The methods of husbandry and the condition of the Scottish rustic as depicted in " The Gentle Shepherd " were the tradition of centuries ; they continued almost without alteration to the time of Burns, who was reared under their influence ; and they survived him for about half-a-century, to a period quite within the memory of living men. Half-a-century ago it was unnecessary to annotate the poems of Burns for country folks : it is necessary to do so now for the present generation of rustics. It is less that his language is growing obsolete, than that the customs more or less closely connected with husbandry and rural life to which he makes such frequent reference are dead or fast decaying.

The condition of the rustic fifty years ago may be partly inferred from the income of an

ordinary able-bodied ploughman.   His year's
fee in money came to ten or eleven pounds;
and there was the provision of milk and meal,
and the shelter of a roof found for him in
addition.   He received from his master two
pecks (old measure) of oatmeal per week, and
one pint (Scots) of new milk per day.   The
home of the unmarried ploughman was the
bothy or the stable-loft.   A house, or rather a
hovel, in the neighbourhood was found for the
married ploughman.   Its annual value, over-
estimated at £2, was subtracted from his fee,
which accordingly amounted to the miserable
pittance of eight or nine pounds.   The hut
consisted of two small apartments—a *but* or
common room, and a closet without a fire-
place, known as the *ben*.   In the common room
or kitchen were two fixed, or box bed-cases,
the backs of which formed the partition wall
between *but* and *ben*.   Attached to the hut
was a small kailyard, in a corner of which
stood a wooden *cruive*, roofed with sod, for
the accommodation of a pig.   There was,
further, the allowance of some land for potatoes,
and it was understood that some field-work
would be found for the ploughman's wife in
the course of the year.   Twenty-six was the
age at which a ploughman usually married,
and he found his wife on the farm.   Trained
to indoor work before marriage, she took her

place after marriage among the field workers,
hoeing turnips, etc., at eightpence a day.   It
would have taken it all to keep her in food,
and meanwhile the care of her own house was
neglected.   There was often, almost necessarily,
little tidiness in or around the house of a
married ploughman.   Of course milk and meal
came to the house just as when the ploughman
had been a bachelor living in a bothy.   These
were all the sources of income of the household.
Himself and wife were "thus sustained," along
with, in the great majority of cases, "a smytrie
o' wee duddy weans."   But the "weans" were
early put to work to relieve the pressure of
indigence.

The unmarried ploughman had fewer cares
than his married brother; but he found the
bothy system of life at times sufficiently cheer-
less too.   Bothies were chiefly on the larger
farms, but they were occasionally to be found
on farms small enough to be worked by two
pairs of horses.   Both man and master (or, at
least, mistress) preferred the bothy to the farm
kitchen, on account of the greater freedom it
permitted to all parties.   Its discomforts, however, were great, even when warmed and lit up
of a winter night by a roaring fire, and enlivened
by the hilarity of hardy young peasants.   They
sat on forms before the fire, or on their own
chests against the wall.   There was in most

cases neither chair nor table. The only other furniture was the beds, which they "made" for themselves—or left unmade, and for which they had the luxury of clean sheets once a month. You passed at one step from the interior into the weather outside; there was no hallan - wall to protect the doorway. It should be added that the bothy was usually infested with rats.

The ploughman of to-day is much better off than was his predecessor in the first half of the century. He has double money, with the same allowance of milk and meal, and his coals are *ca'd* or driven for him free from the nearest railway station. Many ploughmen are now paid a weekly wage, on Saturday nights, of about seventeen shillings; but this money includes everything except house rent in the way of income. The farmer still provides the shelter of four walls and a roof. A soldier's lot is often compared with that of a ploughman. It must be confessed that in ordinary times the advantage is with the soldier. He is better housed, clad, and fed; he has the pretty sure prospect of a pension; and even his mental condition is cared for. From the moment the ignorant recruit joins the regiment he is put to school. The ploughman, it may be said, has greater freedom of individual action; but the value of freedom lies in its use.

The compulsory clause in the Education Act provides the young rustic of to-day with at least the elements of education; but fifty years ago there was no such provision, and the smallness of the ploughman's fee scarcely permitted an elementary education for his children. As a matter of fact the ploughman of those days could read and write with difficulty, if at all. He belonged to a class that may fairly be described as very ignorant. They were ignorant even of farming, though their life was spent in doing farm-work. Their accomplishments were confined to holding the plough, *ca'ing* the harrows, and filling dung. In too many instances they were, in the language of an old farmer who had much experience of them, "as ignorant as the beas' they drave afore them." Ploughmen were a well-defined caste of the community, the direct descendants of the ancient serfs of the soil. How could ploughmen's sons be other than ploughmen? At the tender age of nine or ten the little rustic was put to such field service as he could perform, beginning life as a herd. He had scarcely any—certainly no regular—education after that age. There may have been now and then, for the next three or four years, a quarter's schooling in winter; but what was learned then was soon forgotten. At sixteen or seventeen the growing lad, now a *halflin*, would be promoted to the charge of managing a pair of horses. At eighteen and twenty he was a young giant, possessed of almost incredible strength, tearing and sweating at his toil, and drawing upon his energy with wasteful recklessness. He took no care of himself. It was a mark of effeminacy sure to be ridiculed if he took any precaution against bad weather for the sake of his health or comfort. Wet with rain, and warm with perspiration, the fatigued rustic flung himself down to rest anywhere, and just as he was: like Cowper's hardy chief, "fearless of wrong." The inevitable result was permanent stiffness of the limbs at twenty-eight or thirty. At that age he could not run; he only *hobbled* when he tried. He was an old man in appearance and physical feeling at forty—often at that age abandoning the plough for the spade and pick-axe, the furrow for the drain. He complained of being "ill with the pains," *i.e.*, rheumatism and kindred ailments. His old age, prematurely attained, was "filled wi' grips an' granes.' At forty-five, on the testimony and in the words of Burns, life's day to the battered ploughman was "drawing near the gloaming":

> " For, ance that five-and-forty's speel'd,
> See, crazy, weary, joyless Eild,
>   Wi' wrinkled face,
> Comes hostin', hirplin', owre the field,
>   Wi' creepin' pace."

It was an age to which the ploughman poet was not himself to attain, but he had only to open his eyes to witness the melancholy truth in the experience of his rustic neighbours. And even in his twenty-eighth year he had a personal feeling of the premonitions of age, which he expressed in a peculiar pathos, for it is both tender and despairing :

> " Ye tiny elves that guiltless sport,
>   Like linnets in the bush,
> Ye little know the ills ye court,
>   When manhood is your wish !
> The losses, the crosses,
>   That active men engage !
> The fears all, the tears all,
>   Of dim declining age ! "

The "tiny elves" of this affecting address are of course the young rustics, the "toddlin' wee things" of the cottars of his own neighbourhood. The language is certainly remarkable in the mouth of a young man, but it must not be forgotten that at twenty-eight he had already performed the work of mature manhood for fully fourteen years. His case was not an exceptional one.

One of the advantages of field-work to the necessitous poor—an advantage which secured for it, though the coarsest and humblest of occupations, a plentiful supply of service—lay in the fact that it constantly offered employment to very young children. The pay might

be very small ; but the penny-fee even of the
herd, or the still more diminutive urchin who
could only "run a canny errand to a neibour
toun" (*i.e.*, farmstead), was an addition to the
slender gains of the poor household which the
mother—the manager in such cases—knew how
to put to economical use. The pay, of course,
increased duly with the growing strength of the
young peasant ; but even at its best it must be
acknowledged to have been an inadequate
remuneration when the hardships of a ploughman's lot are considered. Often, in the winter
season, the ploughman's work was simply
terrible.* He had to be out and about even
when his horses could not go without serious
injury. His horses were really better cared for
than himself. When through severity of weather
they were resting in the stable, work was found
for him out of doors : there was manure to be
spread, there were sheep-flakes to be shifted,
there were turnips to be pulled. He was
fortunate if in these circumstances he was put
to such indoor labour as went on in the barn.
Dichting or winnowing the corn was not such
pleasant work as an onlooker might imagine.
It was often the last resort of toil in a thoroughly

---

* It was better world for the ploughman when, in happy
Horatian times, while his oxen rejoiced in their stalls, he
stretched his feet to the fire and dozed through the winter :
gaudet arator igni.

wet day. With his clothes well soaked by the forenoon showers, and badly dried on him at the fire, the ploughman found riddling among barn *stoor* (dust) a by no means comfortable afternoon occupation. But it was something to have escaped the black rains that were lashing field and roadway.

He was called at five in the morning. The foreman was the first person stirring on the farm. His first duty was to waken the bothy. Thereafter he took his orders for the day at the farmer's bedside, if he had not already received them overnight. The master communicated with the men through him. If anything went wrong on the farm, it was he that bore the *dirdum*—as it was called. His first task was to "meat the horses"; each was given a measured allowance of corn or hay. While his cattle munched and digested their meal he *mucked* (cleansed) the stable, and used the curry-comb. It was six o'clock when this was done. For the next three-quarters of an hour he was employed at some outdoor job or other, according to the season of the year, such as . delving "the yard," taking a stack into the barn, or cutting (and carting home) a couple of loads of grass. There was always work to his hand. Then, at 6.45, he made and ate his breakfast of *brose*. He got the hot water at the farm-kitchen, mixed it with the salted oatmeal, upon which it was poured in the thick wooden *caup*, or bowl, by simply describing the figure eight with the end of his horn-spoon, and not seldom ate the unsavoury mess on his way to the bothy. The brose-caup was never washed ; Jock believed that to wash it made the brose *wersh* (*i.e.*, insipid). It may be added that the expression *brose-caup* was sometimes jocularly applied to the ploughman himself : at the feeing market the question was a rather coarse but common one, "How are the brose-caups selling the day?" which being interpreted meant, "How are ploughmen feeing? what wages are they asking?" The ploughman carried his hot caup from the kitchen *suo more*, on his open palm. It was allowed to strike with a spoon the thumb that came over the caup rim. He was no ploughman that could not carry his hot brose-caup in his *loof*. A handful of oatmeal—Jock insisted on being supplied with the very best, and he was a connoisseur—was sufficient to make a diet. He washed it down with a jug of "sweet" milk. The ploughman was so liberally provided with milk and meal that he could afford to save and sell a good deal of the allowance. Brose was his food at the three diets of breakfast, dinner, and supper. The effect of the heating oatmeal diet from day to day was to send out an eruption of boils in the spring.

Without sweet milk to temper the fiery grain, brose could never have been the established and favourite food it is among Scottish peasants. The horses were yoked at seven, and field-work on the farm began. At ten, as the name indicates, their ten-hours' bite was "dealt through among the naigs."

Field-work was dropt at noon for a two-hours' rest. The time taken up in coming from work, even at an out-lying field, was included in the two hours; but the hind and his horses did not leave the stable-door to resume their toil till two. The horses were commonly watered on their way home; but some farmers would permit their horses to be watered only on the way to their work, and after they had had their corn and hay (or grass). If very much heated, the horses would show their enjoyment of the cooling element by thrusting their heads into the water-trough up to the eyes. Old steadily trained horses knew when twelve o'clock came as well as the men themselves; they would indicate their disinclination to exceed the allotted spell of work by turning their heads significantly at the end of the furrow, and whinnying interrogatively. The men slept after dinner for an hour (till two); it was near one when they took their brose. They boiled their own water then. Occasionally in summer their midday meal was milk and

G

part of a wheaten loaf. Their oatmeal went in exchange for the loaf. The afternoon "yoke" was from two till seven. If engaged all day in the laborious toil of cutting with the scythe, the ploughman was allowed half-an-hour's respite in mid-afternoon (and mid-forenoon as well), with the refreshment of scones and cheese, and a drink of small ale sent to him as an extra from the farmhouse. If he was ploughing, the peasant was not allowed this indulgence. It was necessary in that case to keep the horses going. Jockie was therefore obliged to console himself in the furrow with a snuff or a song. Few ploughmen smoked fifty years ago. Farmers did not care to engage smokers ; their carelessness might set fire to the "town." The snuff-box, carried in the breeches pocket, was of the tankard kind— to keep the contents from the wind. The pinch was conveyed to the nose by means of a bone snuff-spoon or *pen*, as it was called. All ploughmen snuffed. Burns speaks as if the ploughman's day in his time was eight hours long—measured doubtless from eight to twelve, and again from two till six. The area of ground broken by a capable ploughman and his pair in the eight hours was certainly good at an acre and a half. But the amount of work done would be greatly determined by the nature of the soil. Stiff clay soil, such as Ayrshire

scarcely knows, would hinder the plough. "Aft
thee an' I," says the Auld Farmer in the famous
and delightful *Salutation*—

> "Aft thee an' I, in aucht hoors' gaun,
>   On guid March weather,
> Hae turned sax rood beside oor han'
>   For days thegither."

An acre of carse-land, such as lies in Strathearn
or the Lothians, would have been as great a
task to turn over as the "sax roods" here
spoken of. Whatever may have been the
length of the ploughman's working day in the
time of Burns, fifty years ago it was ten hours.
Even on holidays and market days, when Jock
had been treating himself to a "spree" in the
"burgh's town," he was almost invariably home
in time to be ready and fit for work next
morning at five. A "late" ploughman was
hardly known; he would have been set down
as *weirdless*, something worse than worthless.
He knew the benefit and the necessity of a due
amount of regular sleep. Ill-health was very
rare with him, thanks to a regular way of life,
plain fare, and plenty of exercise and fresh air.
If he fell ill in service he stayed in the bothy at
his master's charge till he was better, but not
for a longer period than six weeks. The washing and mending of the bothy ploughman, it
may be noticed here, were at his own expense.
A cottar wife in the neighbourhood would keep

him in whole stockings and a clean shirt a week for £1 a year.

The ploughman had few holidays. There was no difference to him between Saturday and Monday. But on Sunday (which he very properly called "the Sabbath") he was free from toil—unless, indeed, it was his turn to wait on the horses. He went to church, or visited his friends or his "folk" (his relatives); very seldom did he stay at his bothy home. All ploughmen, after attaining manhood, were members of some church or other. When the minister paid his pastoral visit to the farmer's family (which he usually arranged to do at mid-day) the ploughmen were called in, and for about half-an-hour were catechised on the principles of their faith as these are set forth in the Shorter Catechism. The ploughmen did not greatly like being examined: they did not relish the exposure of their ignorance. The great secular holiday in the ploughman's year was Hansel Monday, held on the first Monday of the New Year (old style). The summer holiday was the feeing market day. Foremen were engaged at midsummer. The ordinary ploughmen were fee'd for the year in October at the principal market town in the district. There was a market of cattle and horses at the same time, and the day was often enlivened by athletic games or horse-racing. Of course feeing-day was a red-letter day in the ploughman's calendar. It made a great stir in the country side. Jock was elate at the prospect of receiving his money, and was hopeful of an increase for next year, or of a more comfortable or convenient place, or of kinder or more desirable neighbours. A rather cynical old farmer — poor fellow! he never possessed the means to be generous—used to say of his men : " Meal-day an' Marti'mas, it's a' they ken or care!" A young ploughman sometimes did not know when he was well off—as ploughmen went. He would change his service from mere restlessness, and not seldom to his own disadvantage. He would stay because a crony was staying ; he would leave because his sweetheart was leaving. At the feeing market the foreman helped the farmer to pick out the new men. " Are ye gaun to fee?" was the question with which a man in the market might be accosted. He would probably be taken into a public-house near by, if he seemed a likely fellow, and treated to part of " a gill," or a bottle of ale. " Where was he now?" and " How long had he been there?" would be among the next questions. He was never asked why he was leaving. If a bargain was struck, a white shilling of earnest money was put into his hand. Jock called this his *arles*. There was no written agreement, and never (or so seldom as to excite the interest of every farm in the county) any dispute about the fee. The day before the feeing market, or at latest on the market morning, the farmer would ask his men, if he was pleased with their record of service, whether they were " gaun to bide again ? " Those who were content to stop had their holiday about a fortnight after the feeing market. It happened that a ploughman giving up his place failed sometimes to find another at the feeing market ; or a master discharging his men was unable to get substitutes. Provision was made for these cases on the Friday succeeding the Martinmas term. Occasionally that was a great feeing-day, especially if the men were hanging out for an advance. If at last Jock was so unfortunate as to fail to get the fee he wanted, and to refuse less, he would take to knapping stones at the roadside, or to draining, or dyking, or quarrying, or he would become a mason's labourer, or engage to do orra work—*i.e.*, odd jobs about a farm, or in short take a hand in any work that was " going about." Some ploughmen, falling accidentally into this way of earning a livelihood, came to prefer it to serving for a year's fee.

A ploughman's highest accomplishments were sowing and stack-building. To sow well he required to keep two objects steadily in view— economy of the precious seed and utilisation of every square inch of the soil. The prime object of stack-building was to guard the harvested sheaves under "thack and rape" from the damaging assaults of wind and weather. The young ploughman, ambitious to learn the highest mysteries of his craft, practised the art of sowing by scattering handfuls of chaff (or grass seed) in the barn under the eye of an experienced brother.   In building sheaves in the yard into a stack, he was taught to slope the straw just a little from the heads, or ears.   A ploughman who was bad at this work might soon ruin his master, by laying the sheaves so that rain got into the stack and rotted the grain.   A ploughman's talk at the kirk door of a Sunday, where he met his brethren of the district, was seldom about the sermon, or politics either; he talked about the progress of work on the different farms around him, scarcely ever about the crops. The condition of the crops was his master's care, not his.   It was enough for him to "plant" and "water;" the "increase" gave him no anxiety.   His work done, he recked not of the crops.   His questions would run: "Got a' your ley turned owre yet?"   "Muckle o't the 'ear?"   "Are ye lattin' yon chield forrat to the seed-fur this 'ear?"   "He'll be haddin' a gude seed-fur by noo?" etc.   Jock knew nothing about the price of cattle; he was no market man.   Even of farm work he knew

nothing, as a rule, beyond what lay certainly
to his own hand.   He had great pride in his
horses, and liked to boast about having charge
of "a pair o' greys ahint the door that could
rend rocks."   Their strength he regarded as
almost a personal attribute.   He took pleasure
in decorating them on special occasions, such
as ploughing matches, with bits of gaudy
ribbon—red and yellow.   He was kind to
them, unless he lost conceit of them.   He
would steal corn for them; so well was this
known that the foreman kept strict guard of
the corn-chest, which was carefully locked
except when the "feeds" were being served
out—an operation which the foreman super-
intended.

The ploughman's general talk in the bothy
with his associates on the same farm was
sufficiently trifling.   A good deal of it was
about love adventures, intrigues with the vestals
of the kitchen, misunderstandings with the foreman, quarrels with his rivals, and his cattle.
Here and there, there was a reader among
the ploughmen, who would burn a candle at
his own charge far into the night, fascinated
with the exploits of wight Wallace or the
wanderings of Prince Charlie.   He would read
the bothy asleep, and would whisper just one,
and sometimes just one other, chapter to himself.   But Jockie's commonest conversational

diversion was his sweetheart or his cattle. We have Milton's warrant for supposing that the peasants of ancient Bethlehem whiled away the waiting hours in a manner exactly similar; they

> " sat simply chatting in a rustic row :
> Perhaps their loves, or else their sheep,
> Was all that did their silly thoughts so busy keep."

The ploughman had his grievances, both general and particular. A general grievance was the "suppering" of the horses every night at eight o'clock. Jock objected that it "broke his forenicht," and tied him to the farm. Bad meal or milk was a grievance sharply resented. If both were bad on any farm there was insurrection, followed by anarchy, till pardon was asked and amendment promised by the farmer's wife. If there was no redress a rustic bard set the grievance in a ballad, and it flew along the braes like wildfire. Those grievances that were metrically expressed had free vent in ale-houses and whisky-booths at fairs. A specimen or two, frail and fragmentary with long handling, but genuine so far as they go, may prove interesting to some of my readers. Take first the grievance of *sowens for sap*. It should be premised that Jockie preferred *milk for sap* to his brose or porridge, and justly felt aggrieved to be put off with the sour steepings of corn

husks.   The   introductory   lines   are   clearly
wanting :

" We have here a halflin, he says he comes fra Perth,
  An' he's as queer a shaver as ever trampit earth,
  For ilka day wi' Sandy* he has a Waterloo ;
  But sowens for sap on this new taft, my boys, will never do.

" The fourth pair on this new taft, there's one they call 'the
    bay' ;
  The little horse that goes with him, he's true an' trusty ay ;
  Ye'll ken the lad that drives them, he holds the iron ploo—
  But sowens for sap in this new taft, my boys, it winna do !

" We have here a maid for the feedin' of oor nowte,
  And ye may search the coonty ere her marrow ye find out ;
  She is both strong and healthy, an' takes her brose, I troo ;
  But sowens for sap in this new taft, she swears it winna do ! "

Imagine Jockie at the fair, "planted unco richt
beside reaming swats that drank divinely," leading in full enjoyment of his grievance the chorus
of a sympathetic band of "brawny, bainy"
brethren, their sunburnt cheeks lit up with
the sparkle of black eyes and the flash of
teeth whiter than the milk for the restoration
of which on that now notorious "new taft"
they were making such vigorously vociferous
stand.   It was the apotheosis of grief-stricken
Jockie.   His triumph atoned for the past insult
of insufferable sowens.   True he would go back
that very evening to sowens, and a sleeved

---

* Probably the foreman.

waistcoat, the uniform of his toil. To him for the meanwhile, however momentary, the glory of pearls and plush, sympathetic surroundings, and a choral song. But let us look more in detail at Jockie's holiday rig-out. His blue jacket, laden with mother-of-pearl buttons, large, white, and round as infant moons, cost him—if he was honest with his tailor—some fifty or sixty shillings. His vest of red, or yellow plush, cost him close on a pound, and was also resplendent with useless buttons—like Keats's *Lamia*, "full of silver moons." His trousers of corduroy, skin-tight at the knee, fell in loose fetlocks around his ankles. His bonnet was blue, and broad, and kept in aboriginal shape and size by a cane hoop concealed in the lining. A bunch of ribbons, black, but sometimes of mingled blue and scarlet, "streamed like a meteor" at his bonnet lug. Altogether he was "a phantom of delight" unknown to the rising generation.

Among the "grievance" songs may be included those long strings of stanzas descriptive of the hardships of a ploughman's life which used to be chanted at markets and fairs. One of these had for refrain :

"Sad times for us boys amon' the frost and snaw."

Another bewailed the slavish drudgery of the

ploughman's lot on some particular farm, belonging, let us say, to Nabal :

> " Nabal's wark is ill to work,
>   Nabal's wages are but sma',
> Nabal's 'oors are double strict,
>   An' that does grieve me warst of a'.

> " Every mornin' up at five,
>   To kaim wir horse an' keep them clean ;
> But by-an'-by I came to know
>   It was hard wark to serve the freem'd."

It occasionally happened that Jockie got rid
of his grievances at the fair by taking counsel
with the recruiting sergeant.   This myrmidon
of Mars knew that the most likely time to
entice Jockie into the ranks was when he was
fu', and full of grievance.   Jockie's wail of
regret, on his recovery of sense and soberness
at the barracks, might come wafted back to
the green braes he had abandoned in some
such strain as the following :

> " O yesterday was Mononday,
>   That I went to the Fair ;
> I had no mind o' 'listing
>   Till ance that I cam' there.

> " But my heart was full of liquor,
>   And I had no mind of you,
> Or I never wad hae 'listed
>   To the orange and the blue."

BURNS AND HIGHLAND SCENERY.

IT is a common charge against the English poets of the eighteenth century that they were insensible to the wilder charms of nature. Their main object was society; and when they wandered from it, it was to nature as made presentable for society. The charge is true enough of that section of them which includes Pope, Addison, and Goldsmith. Pope looked upon nature with the eyes of a landscape-gardener; and indeed he was one without taking pay. Addison's rambles into the country were the walks of a pensive scholar "on the dry, smooth-shaven green," or

> " with retiréd leisure
> In trim gardens taking pleasure."

Goldsmith got beyond the garden and the lawn, but not beyond cultivated nature and the life of the village farm. He found rustic life poetical only at such a distance as softened its mingling notes. It is an almost impossible effort to think of Addison or Goldsmith in the savage wilderness, surrounded by rocks, and wilds, and waterfalls untamed by art, and untameable. It would be half-ludicrous and half-pathetic to imagine them on the Moor of Rannoch, or let down in the gloom of Glencoe! And yet they actually were in such a situation, for they both crossed the Alps. The personal effect of their experience was characteristic of their genius. Addison shuddered and shut his eyes all the way, and, when they brought him to the mountain-foot, fell on his knees and piously thanked Providence for having, in a meta-phorical sense, warmed the hoary Alpine hills for him. He meant no more than that he was glad he had got over without being frozen to death. Goldsmith kept his eyes open, it is true, for he was on foot and had to beg his way; but he saw nothing but bleakness and barrenness—the hills afforded no product which his poetical faculty could utilise, and his starv-ing muse was fain to make the most it could of a cottage interior at supper time. Still there were poets in the eighteenth century who, though trammelled by the conventional phrase-ology which Dryden invented and Pope popu-larised, saw vividly and felt keenly the wild graces of pagan nature. Of these were Thomson

and Gray. The testimony of Thomson's rap-
turous delight in nature in all her phases is
broadcast in his poetry. Gray's confessions of
his love are in his letters. He may be said to
have anticipated Wordsworth's devotion to the
Lake district. But he, too, was an Alpine
traveller, and appreciated the dread sublimities
around Mont Blanc with all the rapt enthusiasm
of Coleridge and much of the unrestrained
passion of Byron. He wrote home in joyful
distraction of the scene as "solemn, romantic,
astonishing." He could not take ten steps "without an exclamation that there was no restrain-
ing." Where Goldsmith had only shivered,
and Addison had shut his eyes, Gray found
himself in a heaven of poetry and religion.
"Not a precipice," he wrote, "not a torrent,
not a cliff, but is pregnant with religion and
poetry." Little of this vehement joy in the
sterner aspects of nature comes out in the
exquisitely artistic poetry of Gray, and but for
the evidence of his letters it would probably
have been denied to him.

Was Burns of a less robust genius than Gray?
Gray's faculty was much robuster than it is the
fashion to give him credit for, but Burns was at
least no less robust. He lived, besides, in the
freer end of the century, and, thanks to the
traditional usage of his country's poets, had
found in the peasant speech of his day a readier,

if rougher, vehicle for poetical sense and sentiment than was provided in the conventional
metres of the French school, which yet, it must
be confessed, he so much admired. He was
neither likely to quail before such sublimities as
had inspired Gray with unwonted admiration,
nor to refuse to the inspiration, when it came,
the full freedom of such metrical expression as
he was master of. Now his tour in the Highlands brought him face to face with some of the
wilder phenomena of natural scenery, and it
has been argued from his comparative silence
on the subject of Highland scenery, that he was
either insensible of the occasion or incapable of
rising to it. The same charge might have been
brought against Gray if it had not been for the
testimony of his letters. But the extreme
sensibility of Burns to the beauty and grandeur
of uncultivated nature is beyond dispute. It is
found or implied in almost every poem he has
written. The pen that could describe the
thunderstorm in "Tam o' Shanter," the snow-
storm in "A Winter Night," and the anticipated
ruin of the new brig in "The Brigs of Ayr,"
could deal congenially and competently with
Highland gloom and mountain cataract. And
where is the artist that could correct or intensify
the scenery of the Scottish burnie which these
lines present ?—

> " Whyles owre a linn the burnie plays,
>   As through the glen it wimpl't ;
>   Whyles round a rocky scaur it strays ;
>   Whyles in a wiel it dimpl't ;
>   Whyles glitter'd to the nightly rays,
>   Wi' bickering, dancing dazzle ;
>   Whyles cookit underneath the braes,
>   Below the spreading hazel,
>   Unseen that night."

But Burns was not so silent as is supposed on the subject of Highland scenery. The fragment in English on the scenery at Taymouth, whatever its poetical merit, proves at least that he was not blind to the wild graces which there opened on his view. The Birks of Aberfeldy were sung in no unworthy strain. It was no uncritical eye that discovered the only want to make perfect the scenery of the Bruar, and that perceived the peculiar features of the speeding stream :—

> " Here, foaming down the shelvy rocks,
>   In twisting strength I rin ;
>   There, high my boiling torrent smokes,
>   Wild-roaring o'er a linn."

The verses on the Fall of Foyers, near Loch Ness, "written with a pencil on the spot," are a suggestive and powerful sketch of the scene. These, and a few songs which are set in a suggested background of Highland scenery, constitute the poetical outcome of his Highland tour. But the wonder is not that he produced so little, but rather that he produced any poetry at all in the course of his hurried run through the Highlands. Just consider the manner and the circumstances in which he made acquaintance with Highland scenery. It was in August and September of 1787, in the company of Nicol of the High School, an exacting and —in a poetical sense at least—a degrading companion. It was, further, in the rapid course of a tour, lasting in all three weeks, of a by no means private nature. Wherever the poet went there were persons in the neighbourhood that must be visited, and invitations that could not be refused. There was, in short, the intrusive and exacting chat of Nicol, varied by his no less intrusive sullenness and taciturnity, in constant association, relieved — it must have been ordinarily a dreary yet not unwelcome relief—by formal dinners and familiar drinking-bouts every other day. The dinner-in-honour was usually preceded by a visit to the nearest place of common interest—in many cases a waterfall, and Mr Burns was eagerly scanned by his host and party for the revelation of the poetical process, while he scanned the cataract for a poetical idea. He was expected, like Aaron's rod, to blossom into poetry as they gazed, and his patrons would feel defrauded by the poet if the blossom was not forthcoming. Could any thinking man have been legitimately

surprised if in these circumstances Burns had
been poetically silent on the scenery of the
Highlands? He had neither choice of subject,
nor leisure for communion with the spirit of
the scene, nor time to arrange and elaborate
his musings. They led him to the local lion,
and waited for his opinion. He could not
think of the lion for their chatter, and for the
very intrusion of their presence. Once at least
he broke out into vulgar but vigorous indigna-
tion at their senseless conduct. A self-elected
guide was pointing out the capabilities of a
scene for poetical treatment. Mr Burns listened,
and looked on stolidly. A lady of the party
ventured to ask him if he had nothing to say
about the scene. "How can I, madam," he
exploded, "while that ass is braying over it!"

On his return from the Highlands he had
little of the tranquillity necessary for the
poetical recollection of his tour. Other scenes
demanded his attention, other subjects lay to
his hand. For Burns's mind was of that
impulsive and creative kind that does not
travel far for a subject. Given the external
conditions requisite for its treatment, he took
the nearest. Rarely, perhaps only once, did
his muse revert to the Highlands after his
settlement in Dumfriesshire. This was when
the tragedy of Culloden crossed his recollection.
"The Lovely Lass of Inverness" was the birth

of this recollection. Here probably, slight though the lyric is, may be found a hint of the true reason of Burns's comparative silence on the impressive scenery of the Highlands. He could paint landscapes, but he was neither primarily nor essentially a landscape painter. Human figures, historical or feigned, and the interest arising from human associations, were his indispensable subjects. The beauties and sublimities of scenery he utilised as accessories to his main design. He grouped them around the central interest of human association. He believed with Gray—at least he practised the belief—that description of natural scenery made the most graceful ornament of poetry, "but never ought to make the subject." He therefore subordinated the wild scenery of Drumossie Moor to the lament of the imaginary Highland girl who had lost her lover in the battle of Culloden. It is vain to urge that the Highlands are full of romantic memories and heroic associations. These associations and memories were comparatively unknown to Burns. He knew something about Ossian, but, "warm as he was for Ossian's country," where he had "seen his very grave," the "fishing towns and fertile carses" of Banff and Moray drove the enthusiasm from his heart. He was interested in the story of King Duncan, and had pointed out to him the room in which tradition has placed the scene of the tragedy, but the subject was sacred to the genius of Shakespeare. There remained the Jacobite episode in Highland history, and upon that he touched. The romance which now invests almost every Highland scene, and which makes Highland scenery so interesting to us, was a later revelation in which Burns did not share.

WHIPPING THE CAT.

IME was, and not so long ago, when whipping the cat was a widely established custom in broad Scotland, habitually indulged in by a certain class of people of all shades of respectability, even by elders of the Kirk, and entirely approved of, nay, encouraged by rural society everywhere. Indeed, it has not yet quite died out, but the practice of it is now altogether confined to regions, or rather nooks, remote from the centres of civilisation, or inaccessible if near. The universal decay of the custom, and its all but universal disuse, afford no evidence that we have grown more sensitively humane than were our forefathers, for whipping the cat was a proceeding in no respect more cruel, whether from malice or mere thoughtlessness, than hanging the crane. Many an innocently joyous party have assembled to hang the crane,

and many a worthy man has actually spent his
lifetime in whipping the cat.

It is time to inform the bewildered reader
that "whipping the cat" was the popular name
for a particular mode of pursuing certain industrial callings. The expression was principally,
and perhaps primarily, used of tailors; and
where the practice still lingers in outlying
corners of the country, the chance of the
practitioner being a knight of the needle is
as ten to one. But Snip, though its most
devoted and persistent follower, had no right
of patent in the method. Such other craftsmen
as shoemakers, saddlers, and joiners occasionally
"whipped the cat" in the prosecution of their
various arts. Quite recently we even heard a
remarkable paraphrase of the expression applied
to the conduct of a dissenting clergyman, whose
income was the subject of rustic conversation.
The reverend gentleman, it appeared, had been
superannuated, with an allowance from his congregation which every one seemed to consider
parsimoniously small. A tailor--there was no
mistaking his profession—sought to qualify the
general commiseration by hastily observing,
" But look what he makes by flogging pouss !"
and went on to reveal the fabulous sums which
the old gentleman earned in the pulpits of his
beneficed brethren.

"Whipping the cat," or more enigmatically

"flogging pouss,"—it is of tailors we must be understood to speak,—was simply a practice of going from farm-town to farm-town, even from cottar-house to cottar-house, and there working for, and meanwhile messing and lodging with, the inmates. It was doing work for people at their houses. But, while this is what the expression practically meant, it must be owned it flings no light upon the metaphor or its applicability to the action which it was supposed to resemble. How was the peripatetic prosecution of a handicraft, in any view of it, comparable to whipping the cat? And what precisely did the term "whipping" in that connection mean? "Whipping" nowadays has two meanings, the relation of which to each other it is not difficult to make out. The primary meaning is, of course, plain unpoetical flagellation, or beating. Then, as the power to beat implies some kind of superiority in the possessor, to whip may convey the idea of being superior to, or of excelling. Thus, when the Yankee boasted that his country could whip creation, he meant that it was superior to the rest of creation. But this analysis does not help our speculation much, entangled as it is with the difficulty of the cat. Did the metaphor refer to the tailor's agility in leaping from house to house as superior to that of Tom on a predatory excursion? Or was the reference to the domestication of the tailor as supplanting that of Tabby, and driving her from the fireside? We venture these theories in despair, having no other to offer; and neither of them is satisfactory.

There was no exclusive season for whipping the cat: it went on more or less briskly all the year round. It was, however, most actively pursued for a short while in the spring and for a longer period at what country people called "the back end"—that is, the indeterminate and fluctuating interval on the confines of both autumn and winter. Winter, too, was a busy time. New "haps" and wraps, and the stitching and patching of old ones, were needed to keep out the winter's cold, and in spring some attention to appearance—in the way of light vests, fine ribbons, and fancy buttons—was looked for. The finer art of the tailor was therefore called into use in the spring months, while his heavy and coarser work was in preparing for winter, and keeping his clients from its "icy fangs" when it had come. The tailor's services in the scattered homesteads of his district were bespoken long before they were actually required, and day and date were determined and booked weeks and weeks in advance. The best "booking" on many a farm was the herdboy's memory, who anticipated with lively interest the promised, and sometimes sorely-needed, suit of corduroys or velveteens, which only the tailor's visit could realise. Sartor was expected to keep his engagements to the day, and if possible, to the very hour. He had in general a long list of them, which, as a rule, he scrupulously took in the order due to priority of engagement. His customers, calculating on his coming, made their arrangements for his accommodation accordingly, kept themselves from time to time advised of his whereabouts, and commonly knew at what particular house he was, or would be, at any given time. In this way they kept Snip true to his covenants. He could not evade his promise without scandalising a whole community. It was not he only and his next customer that knew of his movements: the whole countryside followed him in all his wanderings, and with jealous eyes tracked him from bank to brae like a badger.

A sad calamity, more than parochial in its consequences, was the death or disappearance of the tailor when the season of making and mending was at its height. His disappearance, like an eclipse, might be total or partial, and could be traced to a variety of causes. The cause might be permanent migration from the neighbourhood, or periodical dissipation, or the rare phenomenon of a strike. For instance, a forsaken or less favoured region coveted a tailor of acknowledged repute, who was secretly approached, tempted with alluring promises, and surreptitiously translated from the midst of engagements and an area of disappointed and perhaps shivering customers. A call to the minister was scarcely of more moment to the parish than was the abstraction of the tailor. Or the tailor, frail man, had fits of "barley-fever," disastrous enough when they occurred regularly, though in that case they could in a measure be provided against, or, at least, allowed for in a customer's calculations, but terribly aggravating to respectable but ragged people when they broke out at unexpected and critical times. So long as his "drouth" lasted, nothing minatory or persuasive would induce the tailor to lift steel or lay seam. Drinking and draught-playing consumed the solid day. Fighting and drinking disquieted the night and the neighbourhood. Meanwhile the sleeveless coat lay untouched in the corner, or the one-legged trousers hung disregarded on the nail. The interlude, which was not without its comic aspects, usually terminated in a bout with the blue devils of a drunkard's creation—from which Snip emerged pale and repentant, with a squeamish stomach and not seldom piously disposed. The minimum of a month's reformation of conduct, combined with steady industry, might then be counted on, and eagerly was the period of his sobriety utilised. With respect to strikes, they were happily rare. When they did occur they formed epochs. Surely everybody has heard of the famous strike of the three tailors of Selkirkshire in the year one of the running century. Behold, the incidents of its progress are written in the chronicles of Christopher North, the Ettrick shepherd being recorder :—

"The tailor at Yarrow Ford, withoot havin' shown ony symptoms o' the phoby the nicht afore, ae mornin' at sax o'clock—*strack!* 'Twas just at the dawn o' the season o' tailors, when a' ower the Forest there begins the makin' o' new claes an' the repairin' o' auld—the maist critical time o' the haill year. At sax he strack, an' by nine it was kent frae Selkirk to the Grey Mare's Tail. A' at ance, no ordinar claes only but mairrage-shoots an' mur-nins were at a dead staun. A' the folk i' the Forest saw at ance that it was impossible decently to get either mairried or buried. For, wad ye believe 't, the mad body was aff ower the hills, an' bat (*bit*) Watty o' Ettrick Pen! Of coorse he strack; an' in his turn aff by a short cut to the Lochs, an' bat Bauldy o' Bourhope, wha loupit frae the buird like a puddock an' flang the guse i' the fire, swearin' by the shears, as he flourished them roun' his head, an' then sent them into the aiss-hole (*ash-pit*), that a' mankind micht thenceforth gang nakit for him, up to the airm-pits in snaw! . . . Never was there sic a terrible treeo (*trio*)! Three decenter tailor lads, a week afore, ye micht hae searched for in vain ower the wide warld. The strike changed them into demons. They cursed, they swore, they drank, they danced, they focht—first wi' whatever folk happened to fa' in wi' them on the

stravaig (*in their idle wanderings*)—an' then, castin' oot
amang theirsels, wi' ane anither, till they had a' three
black een—an' siccan noses ! . . . An' hoo fared the
Forest? No weel ! Some folk, wi' a strang prejudice
against it, began tailorin' for theirsels, but the result was
baith rideeculous an' painfu', an' in ae case had nearly
proved fatal. It's a kittle (*difficult*) airt cuttin' oot. Dandy
o' Dryhope in breeks o' his ain gettin' up, rashly daured
to ford the Yarrow, but they gruppit him sae ticht at the
cleavin' that he could mak' nae head agains' the watter,
comin' down gey strang, an' he was swoopit aff his feet an'
fished oot mair like a bundle o' claes than a man ! . . .
But a' things yearthly hae an end, an' sae had the strike
—though the tailors didna return to their wark till the
langest day."

A country tailor's professional bounds were
in some cases of considerable extent, wider
even than the doctor's. The inhabitants were
not, of course, " thirled " to any particular tailor,
as they used to be to a district mill, or as
farmers engage to support a local blacksmith
with their custom; but they could not always
help themselves, and were very much at the
tailor's mercy. The two qualifications they
most desiderated in their tailor were residence
in the district, and, along with satisfactory workmanship, fair charges. It may well be imagined
that in requiring good workmanship—" good
trade," as it was curiously called—attention
was directed rather to durable stitching than
to elegant cutting. But even rustics had their
ideas of a good cut and a becoming fit, such as

they were; they had a standard of their own, and created a fashion in which they found comfort.

Whipping the cat, like angling, was in the generality of cases a solitary pursuit. But here and there a knot of tailors might erst have been encountered peregrinating the hill paths from one farm-town to another, or socially domiciled in the commodious kitchen of some substantial yeoman or franklin. The fraternity, readily known from the resident rustic by the outward crook and elasticity of their legs in walking, if by no other sign of figure and deportment, would include the master tailor and possibly as many as three journeymen and an apprentice. A master, a journeyman, and an apprentice were, however, more commonly to be met, and formed a more harmonious company. In very hilly and moory tracts, where a length of whaup-haunted wilderness separated homestead from homestead, the little company of travelling tailors would sometimes be allowed the use of shalties, or long-tailed colts, to convey them to their next anchorage,—"then came each actor on his ass;" but whipping the cat on horseback was rare enough to be regarded as a novelty even among those who most frequently witnessed it, and there was always a good deal of rustic badinage at the mounted tailors' expense, both on their departure from one station and on their arrival at another. They rode leaning either too far back or too far forward—the former attitude indicating a dash of bravado which sometimes brought its exhibitor to the recruiting sergeant, the latter manifesting an excessive timidity which, careless of appearances, was concerned only with safety. There was a good deal of swagger among the younger tailors, but the older ones were douce, and rode, like Chaucer's sailor on the rouncey, round-backed, and "as they could." They carried of course their tools with them, and when their journeys between place and place were long and on foot, the weight of one or two of their trade implements pressed heavily but especially irritantly on the shoulders of the apprentice. For to his lot, by immemorial tradition, fell the transport of Ned, *alias* the Goose, which, being interpreted, signified the large smoothing iron. His too was the lay - board, a wooden instrument shaped in outline like a boot-jack, used by the "craft" for pressing sleeve and other seams upon, under the aforesaid smoothing iron. These were carried in a sack, as a pig is carried, and galled the shoulder-blades of the sumpter tyro-tailor most unmercifully. As a consequence he was continually shifting his burden from the one shoulder to the other, or indulging in a rest and a revengeful exclamation among the

gowans in the rear of his party. Master and
man meanwhile tripped jauntily along in
advance, with the air of the pilgrim who
preferred his penitentiary peas boiled. They
were little encumbered with the weight of the
remaining tools, which consisted only of shears,
thimbles, needles, and a store of threads. The
division of their tools in transit was a standing
joke among tailors,—so much so that it
furnished the ordinary words of reveillé. Thus
the master-tailor's early salutation to his satel-
lites on summoning them in the course of a
cat-whipping expedition to "fresh woods and
pastures new," was formally couched in the
cheerful cry, which penetrated to their attic—
"Up, lads! it's a fine morning! Tak' ye the
guse an' the law-buird. I'll bring a' the rest
o' the tewels mysel!" As a rule the tailor was
not a cloth-merchant. The material upon which
he operated was waiting him at the house which
employed him. It had either been purchased
at some shop in the nearest market town, or
got by barter from some wandering "packie,"—
as the pedlar was called. "Cabbaging" was a
vice which tailors were believed to inherit with
original sin, but it was not easy to cabbage,
i.e., pilfer portions of the customers' cloth, to any
finally remunerative extent during a "pouss-
flogging" tour. It was more conveniently
accomplished *in stativis*,—that is to say, when

the tailor was at home, and the stuff was brought to him there.

During his professional perambulations the tailor was paid, not by the amount of work done by him, but by the length of time expended upon it. The common rate at which his time was assessed in the early part of the century was eighteenpence a day, with bed and board in addition. He insisted upon being well-lodged at night. No barn or outhouse, such as served a gaberlunzie, for him. Snip had a soul above straw with a blanket spread over it, and bargained for the accommodation of a box-bed or four-poster; at the worst a shakedown before the gathered fire. If, as once happened, according to the old song, "he fell through the bed, thimbles an' a'," it was doubtless from excess of desire on the host's part to treat him with a dignity answerable to his wishes, even to the ruin of the venerable relic to which he was at nightfall assigned. As for fare, he lived like a fighting cock. He sat down to a breakfast of ham and eggs with tea, dear though the Chinese leaf then was, and expected a repetition of the same for the afternoon meal. He reckoned himself of a social rank at least equal to that of his employer, even if he were a bonnet-laird, and a cut above the farmer, who from custom or economy was content to blunt his appetite in a bowl of

I

porridge. We have heard indeed of a tailor who was surprised into acceptance of a smoking brose-caup for breakfast in an Ochil farmhouse, and who whistled away his chagrin in the faith of a good dinner that would make amends, till, mid-day bringing him only a renewal of the morning's fare, he lost all patience, and stopping his work and his whistling demanded of the mistress whether she took him for a mavis that she offered him nothing but crowdie? But it was seldom that the tailor's *menu* was not to his liking. He was even of influence sufficient to change the established hour of dining in a farm-town so as to make it square with his custom or convenience. Like fashionable people, the tailor dined later than was the normal habit of the farm community, and the farm community during his residence in their midst adapted their hunger to his ways. The pot which contained the constituents of dinner was raised by means of the black crook-shell to a higher link of the kitchen "swey," or crane, than was in ordinary use, with the effect of putting back the boiling till the tailor's appetite was ready for gratification. Indeed one of the links on the crane-chain depending over the kitchen fire was known as the tailor's link, and to this day when dinner is late in a farm-town, the cook is apprised of her remissness with the mild censure which these words imply, " Ye've surely keepit the pat on the tailor's link the day!" The tailor was on most intimate terms with the good wife, and many a confidential crack they had alone together over the afternoon tea. Not only had he edifying talk on the subject of dress, female as well as male, but he carried news as a cadger carried eggs. He was of course a great gossip, and he was consciously possessed of that power which lodges with the man who has knowledge of the secrets of a countryside. His mode of life and the nature of his work not only permitted but positively compelled his accumulation of family histories. He had sharp eyes to see, a glib tongue to ask, and his light and sedentary occupation allowed him leisure of mind to think. He perambulated the country collecting news and disseminating it with modifications now merely rhetorical, now rather malicious. Like the author of evil, he went to and fro on the earth and walked up and down in it. He was flattered and "made o'," * here to induce him to hide the seamy side of a life with which he had become acquainted, there to induce him to reveal it. The hospitality which he generally experienced he could thus have in a manner enforced. No goodwife could afford to fall out with him, for no goodwife could afford to set his opinion at defiance. Rivalry, secret or avowed,

* Made much of.

was great among farmers' wives in household matters, and the tailor, locomotive among the households, was like a fox with a firebrand among reputations. His tongue could be as sharp as his bodkin. A joiner or other crafts- man whipping the cat, had no such influence or importance, for the simple reason that he was not an inmate-guest like the tailor. The joiner knew the fact well, and could ill brook the sense of his inferiority which it seemed to carry with it. We knew an honest wheelwright, of a calm dis- position by nature, who once "let out" upon the whole fraternity of tailors in a way that astonished us. He was himself whipping the cat at a farm, and "putting up" with the farm fare uncomplainingly, swallowing his porridge night and morning without a murmur, till an itinerant tailor came on the scene. The com- motion made by Snip's advent roused a very demon of jealousy in the wheelwright's bosom. "That cruckit fraction o' a cratur—for he was a' thrawn east an' wast like an izzat—pat the haill toun aboot to serve him!" How the circumstance of the tailor being a cripple should have increased his ire was not quite transparent. It would have been hazardous to point out to him that the tailor was an artist in cloth, and that the heavy meal of porridge which suited the labours of a wheel- wright could not have been worked off so easily on crossed legs and by fingering a needle.

The tailor's stay at any place was of course largely determined by the number of male members in the household. He stayed as long as there was work for him. The period varied from a day to "an eight days." As he was paid by the day his hours were a matter of some consideration. They extended from eight in the morning till six or, in some localities, eight in the evening. Besides the three intervals for diet he had discretionary powers for stretching his legs. During his working hours he was accommodated in the kitchen, usually a roomy apartment, or "ben" the house—that is, in the best room of a cottage. He sat *suo more* on a table-top. Perched occasionally on the narrow disk of a round "claw-table," he gave quite a picturesque effect to the room, looking like an Indian idol set up for worship, or a nodding Chinese mandarin. It was a schoolboy's trick, but dangerous and therefore rarely practised, to withdraw the pin of the table on which the tailor was squatted. The game was christened "Up goes froggie!" The game, it may be added, only began *after* froggie had gone up. It sometimes continued long after that. In the winter evenings, beautifully called in Scotland "the fore-nights," the tailor and his men were in all their glory atop of a large square table

stationed against the long wall of the farm
kitchen. Opposite them was the blazing hearth-
fire which flooded bole and beam within and
above the four corners with light. But candles
were also provided for the tailors, one between
every two of them. Field and outhouse work
were over, and indoor domestic work was well
over too. The maids were at leisure, and the
ploughmen dropped in to look at the tailors,
and to listen and laugh at the queer stories they
were sure to tell. Then was the opportunity of
the tailors. More than any craft, perhaps, they
had an instinct for startling and astounding and
showing off. There was in their words, too, a
sententious smartness which greatly tickled the
ear of Jock Upoland. Their speech and air and
gestures were as good as a play to him. He
roared with delight even when the sarcasm was
pointed at himself, or the story told at his
expense. Of bulkier body than Snip, and of
infinitely less individuality of mind, he seemed
like a great genial Brobdingnagian glowering
with all his eyes at the martial antics of Gulliver.
If any envy of Snip's superiority of address
arose in his mind, it was quickly swamped by
the recollection that he lived in an entirely
different world, which rarely met Snips, or by
the consciousness of possessing greater physical
strength. When he felt the touch of Snip's
satire he would rest content with the revenge of

referring to him as " a nacket," " steek," " prick-
the-loose "—something, in short, that belittled
him, or was supposed to caricature his industry.
It was the ploughman's interest, however, to
keep sweet with the tailor when the latter had
him professionally in hand.   His attractions as
a beau depended materially upon the goodwill
of the tailor ; nay, his success as a wooer, and
therefore the whole of his future happiness, lay
to a large extent in the tailor's art.   Jock was a
striking figure when, under favourable sartorial
auspices, and with health, youth, and fine May
weather in easy auxiliary attendance, he assumed
the part which, according to Shakespeare, we all
pass through, of "braw wooer," and stalked
"down the lang glen" to see his jo.   His fault-
less fawn-coloured corduroys caught him at the
knees and fell loose about his ankles, a knot of
blue and red ribbons danced above his calves,
and mother o' pearl glanced lavishly about his
fetlocks.   His waistcoat was of crimson plush,
and twinkled with rows of starry white buttons,
while his short jacket of mole-black or snuff-
brown velveteen showed in front and at sleeve-
band another display of pearls, but of larger
size—large and lustrous as moons.   His broad
blue bonnet surmounted brows of more than
regal happiness, and was adorned with a rosette
and a whip of gaily coloured streamers, that
rustled in his left lug like the cap-wing of

Mercury. Now all this bravery was the result of the tailor's art. He could make it, he could mar it, he could altogether withhold it. Our picture of Jock's equipment as a wooer is complete when we have put a song in his mouth, a book of ballads in his right hand, and a brass-bound whip under his left arm.

Besides the fun and joking, chat and story in the long winter fore-nights, there would be now and again what Burns in ploughman's phrase calls "a hearty yokin' at sang aboot." Every tailor could sing, and his songs—those, namely, which celebrated his craft — were invariably characterised by a brisk cheerfulness of both sentiment and tune. A pretty popular class-song of his commenced :—

> " Wat ye hoo the wars began,
>   Benjamin jo, my dear ?
> Wat ye hoo the wars began ?—
>   Cast threeds away ! "

When it came to the ploughman's turn to sing, a contrast was usually presented. The plough-man too had his jocular and humorsome songs, which he bawled out with an energy that would well have illustrated the mode of keeping the sum of the ten commandments required by the catechism. With full throat and from a whole heart he roared till kebbars shook and girdle rang, and perhaps a saturnine-visaged shargar of a tailor would problematically suggest that

" a stane was surely in that cuddy's lug." But
as a rule the ploughman's song was tender, even
tearful, of sentiment, with wonderful touches of
true pathos and poetry, making themselves felt in
unexpected places, and set to a simple plaintive
air, which awoke the imagination and haunted
the memory. The cause of such a preference
of songs by the ploughman was somewhat
puzzling to any one who philosophised on the
subject; it seemed so little in harmony with his
vigorous body and healthy, heavy work. Probably those plaintive songs were complementary
to his essentially joyous disposition; and an
instinct for them as for some novelty was
possibly created and developed by the voice of
something sad, that creeps in mysterious under-
tone even through the glad sounds of nature.
Early brought face to face with nature, and
kept continuously in her changeful presence,
the young ploughman soon perceives—

> the wail o' autumn wun's,
> O' trees, an' seas, and settin' suns,
> O' melancholy muirlan' whuns
> And hillside sadness,
> And e'en the greetin' voice that runs
> Through Nature's gladness.

To this day, anywhere in Lowland Scotland
between the braes of Angus and the hills of
Galloway, if a solitary ploughman, old or young,
is overheard whistling or singing to himself

down the new-drawn furrow, the likelihood is
that the tune is the "Flooers o' the Forest" or
the "Bonnie Hoose o' Airlie," or some such
mournful melody. At social gatherings he is
more influenced by the spirit of good-fellowship,
though even then the notes of sadness, so
seldom heard in his speech, will escape from
him in song. There was no such depth, or at
least display of feeling in tailors, considered as
a class.

The itinerant tailor was the theme of many
a rustic song, composed at his expense and
sung in his absence. Amatory escapades, to
which he was rather prone, from a nature
peculiarly susceptible of female charms, were
a favourite subject of those compositions. A
fair representative of this class of songs began :—

> "The tailor cam' to cloot the claes,—
> Sic a braw fellow !
> He filled the hoose sae fu' o' flaes,
> Daff-an-doo, an' daff-an-doo,
> He filled the hoose sae fu' o' flaes,
> Daff-an-doo, and dillow !
> "The lassie sat ayont the fire,
> An' smirkit on her Willie ;
> An' she was a' his heart's desire,
> Daff-an-doo, an' daff-an-doo,
> O she was a' his heart's desire,
> Daff-an-doo, an' dilly ! "

Sometimes his adventures were judged to be
of sufficient interest to merit the dignity of
prose—always greater than that of verse in

rural districts—and to receive a place in chap-book literature. Thus "Lippard the Tailor," the hero of a marvellous "cauf bed," was the title of a popular chap-book story about fifty years ago, as well known along the whole range of the Sidlaws, Ochils, and Campsie Fells as "The Foundling of Dumbarney," or the "Wast Mill Whistler," or " Green Sleeves o' Bamawnie," or "Wise Willie and Witty Eppie," or "The Hind," or "The King and the Cobbler," or a hundred others, coarse but humorous, now forgotten.

But the days of itinerant tailoring are numbered. Readier means of communication between places far apart have superseded his slow and not always certain mode of progress. A wider knowledge of the fashions in dress has made the people among whom he whilom found his clientelage too critical for the support of his art or the composure of his mind. The farmer would now regard him with unkindly eye as a vagrant or "gangrel body," to be warned into the highway, or at best referred to a crevice of the barn till daybreak. Even the frugal cottar would refuse the cheap offer of his services. Jock knows him no more ; he carries his body to the market-town to the measurement of a scientific tailor, and receives his apparel (from which pearls have vanished) with the despatch that characterises the delivery of the Parcel Post.

THE ART OF BURNS.

" Gie me a spark o' Nature's fire !
That's a' the learning I desire."

TOO much is beginning to be made of the art of Burns. A recent writer goes so far as to say that he was the greatest literary artist of last century. Another declares that he was essentially a literary man, detects his artistic instinct in the folds of his philomot plaid, and compares his method in the composition even of his songs to a clever, but merely mechanical, whittling of cherry-stones. Burns, it will be allowed, was more than any man of modern times the poet of the people ; and their opinion, founded on a very intimate and living acquaintance with his poetry, is beyond all question, that he sang very much as natural people speak—freely, boldly, and without the premeditation which the use of art implies. There is absolutely no reason whatever to alter the popular verdict. Burns belongs to the class

of natural poets.* He is of kin to Shakespeare
and Scott, rather than to Pope and Tennyson.
He is of those who "never blotted a line"—
whose song was meant for ears and hearts
rather than eyes and intellect. His station is
in public places and the open air, and he is not
to be confined in closets and class-rooms. He
is for common people, and not for critics. His
utterances were effusions — to restore a word
that has fallen into disrepute. They came
straight from the strongly stirred springs of
inspiration within his poet soul, and abide with
us in their original robustness and freshness and
perfection, unmodified by art and untinkered by
artifice. There they are as he first expressed
them. "I cannot alter them; to the world
they must go as they are," was the motto of his
practice. There is no science in his poetry.
His strains are racy. They are such as should
come from the lips of an inspired ploughman.
Ploughman he was, and not penman. The
instruments he dealt with were flails and pattles,
scythes and seed-sheets — not quills and ink-
horns. He was a literary man in the sense that
what he left us is literature, but in no other.
His were not the literary habits that make

* "I am nae poet *in a sense*—
[I] hae to *learning* nae pretence."
Here "*in a sense*" may stand for "in an 18th century sense;"
and "*learning*" clearly stands for "art."

writing a profession. Pope, who was certainly
not without natural genius, was the first of our
literary or professional poets. His method was
a complete contrast to Burns's. So many lines
were struck off at a sitting, and were then
leisurely operated upon, till, what with prun-
ing and paring, altering and condensing, their
original character was scarcely discernible in the
residue. The result was often effective, but it
was hardly the offspring of inspiration: it was
more the manufacture of art. It drew admiration, but the admiration was rather for the
neatness of the expression than for the native
force or beauty of the idea. Compare with this
process of making poetry the creative manner of
Burns. He demanded first to feel, to appropriate
his theme. He could not, like so many elegant
versifiers, love it and yet keep it at arm's length.
If he loved it, it was caught up into his heart—
ceased to be an object, and became a subject.
There, in his heart, in some over-mastering
passion, the poem began; and thence, and not
from his head, it was propelled in language
hastily caught up as by some magnetic force,
and in the best sense expressive, for it was
animated and informed with soul. The words
" came skelping, rank and file, a'maist before
he kenn'd." Utterance, and not the method of
utterance, was his care. He was reckless of
methods of execution, if only the work was

done. Like his own whisky-inspired Highland soldier, his one thought was to kill "twa at a blow."

Art affects expression only. Of his expression Burns took no conscious care — unless, indeed, as was occasionally the case, he undertook a theme for which he had no heart. The result on those unhappy occasions was usually an exercise in English verse composition on the model of the Queen Anne School. Here the ideas were commonplace, and counted for nothing to either reader or writer ; the language was everything, and alone fixed the attention. It was a laboured composition of conventional phrases; it was Burns's attempt at art, but was rather artifice, and not very clever at that. It was to his native expression what Milton's Italian exercises were to his English poems. It is in his native Scottish that we find the poetry of Burns. Here his words are transparent, and his ideas luminous and glowing. The idea, or the feeling, has etherealised the word, so to say, with the result that word and idea seem to be inseparable and identical. This union of word and thought was not the invention—it was the birthright of Burns. It is characteristic of classical Scotch, and there was classical Scotch before Burns, and even before Ramsay. It is not our purpose here to account for this wonderful union of word and thought—this expressiveness of Lowland Scotch, for that is what it comes to; enough to say that it was already made when Burns in his boyhood learned its force from the lips of his father, and its flexibility from the rustics of Ayrshire. A poetical instinct or intelligence guided Burns in his selections from its copiousness and in his applications of its suggestiveness, which was no more conscious art than is the ordinary practice of speech. Whole pages of the poetry of Burns, as far as the language in which it is uttered is concerned, might be quoted, which were caught up in all their idiomatic purity and power from country roadsides and rustic cottages. Take as a specimen the dialogue between Death and the Poet, introductory to the discussion of Dr Hornbook. The language there, and numerous additional instances might be given, was not more the style of Burns than it was the style of many a mute inglorious Scottish peasant. It was, it had been, and even yet in happily neglected nooks it is, the Scottish style. Those who are ignorant of this, Englishmen and oxidised Scotsmen, will naturally, as has been done, give Burns all the credit of it.

The fact is — and it is still too widely ignored — Burns was not the isolated phenomenon in Scottish literature which Carlyle, followed by hundreds, first proclaimed him to be. The language he has made famous was not to create, but lay already fully formed to his hand; the forms of his verse were already established favourites, thoroughly familiarised to the Scottish ear; even his themes were directly suggested by traditionary usage. His indebtedness to Fergusson and Ramsay, we pointed out at some length in the *Scotsman* newspaper a few years ago.* The remarkable continuity of the Scottish school of poetical thought and expression was then affirmed, and some proof of the affirmation was given. It was pointed out that Ramsay introduced Burns into almost every department of poetry in which he excelled. Burns was a historical development; he was the "bright consummate flower" of a perfectly natural and organic national growth. To the green, or only partially opened, buds of Ramsay and Fergusson his poetry, indeed, offers the contrast of midsummer bloom and fragrance; but it is yet the development of those buds, glowing on the same stem and drawing nourishment from the same soil.

In short, in the mechanical parts of versemaking, Burns imitated the native models with a closeness that is often surprising and little indicative of original art. The purblindness, if

---

* The *Scotsman* articles here referred to were republished in the author's first volume of Scottish Essays *For Puir Auld Scotland's Sake* (W. Paterson, 1887).

K

not dishonesty, of some critics is not more
manifest than when they go into ecstasies
over, for example, the beautiful fitness to the
subject of the stanza employed in "The
Cotter's Saturday Night." It may safely be
said that Burns used that stanza where he
did because Fergusson had used it or something like it in "The Farmer's Ingle," and for
no other reason. Form was of small account
to Burns. Some form, of course, he must use;
but a burnt stick, as Carlyle says, is burin
enough in the hand of a master. There was as
little art, in the ordinary sense of the word, in
his language. It was the language of his every-
day life, the habitual language (only preciously
freighted) of his country; not a thing of search
and selection, but the easy possession of a
second nature. It was with ideas and feelings
that Burns dealt; and expression in all its
forms was with him instinctive, or at most a
secondary, and therefore a successful, thing.
He was careful with his ideas and feelings.
Was man his subject? He represented him
as he saw him, to the life, neither better nor
worse than he is. Was it nature he described?
The one thing he required of himself was truthfulness to his ideal in the representation. A
bold truthfulness to his own views, "uncaring
consequences," was the one task he set himself.
His means for the destined end never distracted

his attention—never distracts his readers; unless, indeed, when we have escaped from the spell of his magic, it is to marvel at the simplicity or rudeness of the wand with which that magic was wrought.

THE DOOM OF VAGRANCY.

" We'll gang nae mair a roving, sae late into the night,
    And we'll gang nae mair a roving, let the moon shine e'er
    sae bright."

VAGRANCY still seems to be an evil of no mean magnitude in Scotland. There is arithmetic to prove it. For the first time in the history of the country a census of the vagrant classes was taken on a day in the Christmas week of 1888, and the result has been made public in a significant circular issued by the secretary of the Chief Constables' Club. There are, it appears, some eight or nine thousand vagrants living by their wits, on the bounty, or at least at the expense, of the settled community. About 5000 of these practise in the rural districts, and considerably over 3000 haunt and sorn upon the towns. The census is correct as far as it goes; it shows the minimum number of the vagrant files; but there is good ground for believing that the official enumeration of professional mendicancy is incomplete.

It is virtually admitted that many members of the gangrel fraternity have eluded the eye of the Chief Constable ; but the eye of the Chief Constable is not done with them yet. He has merely commenced his inspection of their scattered and tattered ranks. In accordance with a regulation of the Secretary for Scotland, he prosecutes a more searching inspection shortly. It is in the wider areas of the country that the difficulty of securing a full enumeration is chiefly felt. Indeed, it is hardly possible that the police unaided can explore all the outlying places where vagrants find a night's shelter, and the assistance of farmers, and other dwellers in the country upon whose skirts the wanderer is wont to alight, has been asked to enable the police to make a full and accurate return of the names, numbers, etc., of our native nomads. More than this, the census is to be taken half-yearly till further orders—that is, till mendicancy is fairly got in the grip of the County Council and shaken out of its rags and its roving into respectability and regularity of life. It is in the following significant terms, in the circular referred to above, that Mr Porter, secretary to the Chief Constables' Club, pronounces the doom of the vagrant :—

" In view of local government by County Councils, and the probability of application being made to obtain power to deal with vagrancy under the bye-law section of the Local Government Bill, it is desirable that the census returns should be as complete as possible to enable the Councils to perceive the magnitude of the evil with which they have to deal."

The contemplation of the suppression of vagrancy will excite mingled feelings of satisfaction and regret. Perhaps no institution, whatever its character, if only it is of long-established usage, ceases to exist without arresting the attention, more or less regretful, of many to whom it has been familiar. The institution of vagrancy has something of the charm of antiquity. It is of venerable date. Not to mention our first parents, who were driven from flowery bowers, a pair of unwilling vagrants over the vacant earth, there is the wandering of Cain, about as ominous a beginning of voluntary vagrancy, it is true, as can well be imagined, but sufficient to prove its high antiquity. From his practice, doubtless, was developed in some of his children that instinct of errancy from which in due time proceeded the three great vagrant tribes of gipsies, tinkers, and strolling fiddlers and pipers. So at least we interpret the Scriptural classification of his wayward children into the dwellers in tents, the workers in brass and iron, and the handlers of harp and organ. But, ingenious though they were, those waifs and strays of primeval man were swept away by the Flood.

Yet the distemperature of mind which produced them survived the great washing. And it is significant that just after the great lustration of the early world a mighty, if rather misdirected, attempt was made to keep the human family from lapsing into the old and evil irregularities of a lax life by the erection of a central tower, which should be the sign and symbol of settlement and social industry. It was a fond attempt, the first fiasco of the renovated world. It was contrary to a habit, if not an inherent principle, of life, which had become in the race a second nature. Mutual repulsion by and by manifested itself among the increasing units of Noah's offspring, and swarm after swarm radiated to all the quarters from the parent hive at Shinar. Each swarm in its turn gave off, as occasion served, a band of independent stragglers, of which the house of Terah may be regarded as a typical example. Of his strain, but on the cold side of the coverlet, came Ishmael, whose erring progeny are vexing the Soudan to-day. Of his strain, too, but in the legitimate line, were the runaways from Egypt, the desert-wandering Israelites. Their roving impulse survived the long indulgence of milk and honey; it re-appeared in the Jews of the dispersion, lives somewhere yet in the Lost Ten Tribes, and is for ever perpetuated in the idea of the Wandering Jew.

So far, then, the antiquity and persistency of
vagrancy have been made out on a Bible basis.
It would be easy to get corroborative evidence
from classical history. Incidentally, in the course
of our all-too-rapid survey it has been shown
that vagrancy can lay claim to a measure of
respectability. It is venerable alike from its
age and the character of some of its practi-
tioners. The respectability of Abraham, for
instance, is above suspicion. It may be objected
that, though he was a vagrant, he was no mendicant. Neither, for that matter, was Ishmael a
mendicant, though a vagrant of a most virulent
type. Abraham did not need to beg, as he had
enough already to support his vagrancy ; and
why should Ishmael beg if he had the power to
take ? There are many shifts by which vagrants
live, and levying blackmail is the certain resource
of the sturdy and needy vagrant. David himself
practised it among the farms of Judah with as
little compunction of conscience as our own Rob
Roy among the hirsels of the Lennox and the
stackyards of Stirling. It is to the weak and
the spent we must look, to find those who, in
the absence of personal resources, must take up
the art and practice of begging by which to
maintain their vagrancy. Your true mendicants
are they. Yet even to them tradition allows
a modicum of respectability. Nay, Fame has
found them out ; the halo of romance has glori-

fied them. Belisarius solicited ha'pence at the roadside, Homer was an itinerant minstrel, and it was a beggar maid that King Cophetua wooed.

In its historical aspect there is thus something venerable in vagrancy. Viewed poetically as a mode of existence, it is far from destitute of charm. It opposes to the laborious confinement and monotony of a settled life the idea of a great freedom, accompanied by diversity of scene and variety of incident. There is neither task to tire the body, nor care to fret the mind ; neither spinning nor toiling, nor thinking of the morrow. Life is mostly "a dandering in fine weather beside bonny burnsides and green shaws " — to employ the figure of a famous Blue-Gown. Nor is the freedom which vagrancy promises that of the limbs only ; it offers immunity from the restraints of convention, and the fear of public opinion. This was the aspect of it that touched the imagination of Burns, and early reconciled him to a life of obscurity and poverty. He anticipated the vagrant life in all sincerity, and took no fright at the view. At the same time he was not blind to the wretchedness and the realism of it :—

> " To lye in kilns and barns at e'en,
> When banes are crazed, an' bluid is thin,
> Is doubtless great distress ! "

But he knew how much he had to fear, and the

effect of that knowledge was to swallow up for the time all fear; he knew how far he could sink, and discounted the humiliation of it long before his usefulness to his kind and his right to toil could have by any possibility been challenged. "The last o't, the warst o't, was only but to beg." He had calculated all the miseries of mendicancy—the gowpen of meal or other awmous, the failing strength and increasing stiffness, the squalor of the kiln-pot shelter or at best the barn, the bed of broom or bracken with the wind for a blanket, even the "cadger powny's death at some dykeside;" he contemplated them all without much horror.* As Scott observes, "he reckoned up with true poetical spirit the free enjoyment of the beauties of nature which might counter-balance the hardship and uncertainty of the life even of a mendicant. The idea of such a life was not ill-adapted to his habits and powers." But there are many ways in which the attractions of vagrancy on its picturesque side can be illustrated. Even kings in a frolic have donned the gaberlunzie's gown, and have gone a-roaming late in the moonlighted night. Those were the palmy days of beggardom. Goldsmith practised in that mad escapade of his on the Continent the mode of

---

* "Even the last worst shift of the unfortunate and the wretched does not much terrify me," etc.—*Letter* (15th January 1783).

life which Burns only anticipated in mind, or
saw as an outsider at Pousie Nancy's. Before
Burns he found that your vagrant is the only
true heir of creation. Then, what a picturesque
figure the vagrant is in literature! Both Shakespeare and Sir Walter have delineated him with
kindly touches. To most of us Autolycus and
Edie Ochiltree are like personal acquaintances,
as life-like as ever were their creators. Yes, it
is sad to think that the class which furnished
such models is to be improved off the face of
the earth. We are getting dreadfully uniform
in our respectability!

The public voice in this utilitarian age is
doubtless for the suppression of vagrancy.
Goldsmith's kindly treatment of "the well-
remembered beggar," Burns's human sympathy
with "randy gangrel bodies," Scott's inevitable
respect for the King's bedesmen, "the aristo-
cracy of their order," Lamb's complaint of "the
decay of beggars," are little likely to find favour
or imitation now-a-days. It may be that only
the dregs of vagrancy are left, and that the
sooner they are cleared off the better for them
and us. But it cannot be denied that the speed
at which the industrious to-day are driven
makes them intolerant of that indolence which
appears to the ordinary mind to be the chief
feature of vagrancy. The present popular
estimate of beggars, at its mildest, is very much

that of Cowper, to whom gipsies were a puzzle; he could not understand why they should "prefer their squalid sloth to honourable toil," more especially as their toil was needed for "the profit of the world." At its severest the public view of vagrancy at present can hardly be said to match that of Fletcher of Saltoun two hundred years ago.

"Those vagabonds," he says, "live without any regard or subjection either to the laws of the land, or even those of God and nature. Many murders have been discovered among them; and they are not only an unspeakable oppression to poor tenants who, to escape insult, must give bread to perhaps forty such villains in one day, but they rob many poor people who live in houses distant from any neighbours. At country weddings, markets, burials, and the like, they are to be seen—both men and women—perpetually drunk, cursing, blaspheming, and fighting together. They create such disorders, that *it were better for the nation they were sold to the galleys or to the West Indies* than that they should continue any longer to be a burden and curse upon us."

These are angry words, but Fletcher did well to be indignant at a state of matters which permitted one-fourth of the entire population to live in vagrancy. The present proportion is not quite one in four hundred.

THE PROSE OF BURNS.

THE world remembers Burns for his verse, particularly for his lyrics. To the world he is a singer of a singularly strong, sweet, and varied note. It is apt to forget that he wrote prose at all. Yet in point of quantity his prose rather exceeds his verse; and as to quality, it has been highly praised, not only on its merits, but relatively to his poetry, by philosopher, historian, and critic, all eminent, and owing much of their eminence to their talent for prose composition. Dugald Stewart found in the prose of Burns "great and various excellences," and declared that some passages were "scarcely less objects of wonder than his poetical productions." Robertson went further—he actually thought that Burns's prose was more extraordinary than his poetry. And one of Jeffrey's many varying dicta on the subject was expressed in the statement that the prose works of Burns bear, as well as his poetry, the seal and impress of his genius. Carlyle, who, in his single self as philosopher, historian, and critic, was of weight perhaps equal to these three, has endorsed their judgment so far as to allow that for the most part Burns wrote prose "with singular force and even gracefulness," and that "whenever he wrote to trusted friends on real interests his style became simple, vigorous, expressive, and sometimes even beautiful." With these facts and opinions before us, and with the knowledge that the prose of Burns frequently deals with "real interests" of universal importance, it is somewhat strange that his prose should be so much neglected. It is also matter of regret. His prose expresses himself more freely and familiarly, more fully and precisely, than his verse. It gives us the every-day Burns—Burns from day to day. It is, if perused in the order in which he wrote it, the best, because the most genuine, biography of him that we can have. Yet it is neglected for histories which present him in imaginary aspects and interpretations which are absurdly at variance with plain fact. Within the last five or six years, for example, the public have been flippantly told that Burns never loved woman in his life ; that if there was one woman more than another whom he despised, it was Jean Armour ; that the composition of his songs was a mere whittling of cherry stones; that he died of being Robert Burns ; and other fearful and wonderful paradoxes. But we need not go so far back; within the last five or six months the young men of Edinburgh have been informed* that the cause of Burns's death was his want of common sense, and that in spite of his great genius he was no better than a fool. It is to be hoped that the number of people who are likely to credit these oracles is limited. The only final corrective of these and kindred extravagances, which really seem to be the product of purblindness, or self-sufficiency, or a lust of paradox, is to be found in that revelation of himself—that autobiography—of which his prose writings really consist. A tolerably perfect idea of Burns as a poet can be gathered from his poetry, and there can be no doubt that it is in his office and function of poet that his countrymen chiefly love to remember him; but to know him as a man and a member of toiling, tempted humanity, we must make resort to his prose writings—the most, if not the only, authentic source of this knowledge which we possess. His prose admits of a twofold but very unequal division into letters and other pieces. The letters make up the great bulk of his prose; the other pieces are a small and fragmentary but motley collection, comprising three journals, kept at Mossgiel, Edinburgh,

---

* By a *University* Professor—it is necessary in these days to discriminate.

and Ellisland respectively ; two itineraries, the one of a tour in the Lowlands, the other of a tour in the Highlands ; notes to two series of Scottish songs ; various prefaces, particularly the remarkable dedication of his poems to the Caledonian Hunt ; a legal document of some curiosity, drawn up by the poet-exciseman in prosecution of a smuggler ; masonic minutes ; inscriptions ; and a few scraps of a nondescript nature.

The published letters of Burns number close upon five hundred and forty. They extend over a period of sixteen or seventeen years, commencing in the end of 1780, with a love-letter to Alison Begbie, when the writer was in his twenty-second year, and ending on Monday, 18th July 1796, with an urgent letter to his father-in-law, when the writer was within a week of the middle of his thirty-eighth year—a point he was never to reach, for he was at the same time within three days of his death. There is thus an average of about twenty-six letters to each year, but the actual distribution ranges from the minimum of one in 1782 to the maximum number of ninety-two in 1788. The first six of the seventeen years of corre-spondence have only fourteen letters among them ; it is in 1786, the year of his literary birth at Kilmarnock, that his correspondence begins to be heavy. In that year the number

of letters written by Burns goes up at a bound
from two in the preceding year to as many as
forty-four. The apparent increase is easily
accounted for: Burns, who from his sixteenth
year had been a voluminous letter-writer, was
now for the first time recognised as a man of
genius—whose letters were therefore worthy of
preservation. The statistics for the remaining
ten years of the period are:—In 1787, 78
letters ; in 1788, 92 ; in 1789, 54; in 1790, 33;
in 1791, 44 ; in 1792, 31 ; in 1793, 66 ; in 1794,
30 ; in 1795, 27 ; and to July 1796, 24 letters.
The average for these ten years is forty-eight,
but there are three years which considerably
exceed it. The first of these, the year 1787,
was a complete holiday year to the poet. The
only business he had on hand was the publication of the first Edinburgh edition of his poems.
He had thus abundant leisure, and the novelty
of his position supplied him with subjects. The
next year may be distinguished as the "Clarinda
year" of his correspondence. His entangle-
ment with that lady added to the epistolary
crop of the year as many as thirty-five letters,
all written in something like ten weeks. The
third unusually productive year is the year
1793, and the cause of its fertility is traceable
to the stimulating proposal of George Thomson
to wed to the best Scottish tunes words that
should match them. The proposal appealed at

L

once to the patriotism and the poetry of Burns's
nature, and he caught it up and carried it to
a successful issue with characteristic ardour.
Twenty - six letters were written in 1793 in
support of the scheme. But the value of the
letters lay in what accompanied them. From
George Thomson he received—he would take—
no money which can at all be regarded as
recompense for his work. But fame is a dearer
guerdon to the poet's heart, and Scottish music
amply repaid Burns for his services by spread-
ing and preserving his name. His songs live
with what is best in distinctly Scottish music.
It is not for their merits alone that they linger
in every memory and live in every mouth, but
they have become identified with their musical
expression so completely, that many people in
our experience believe the tunes, no less than
the words which are sung to them, to be the
composition of Burns.

The number of Burns's correspondents was
significantly large : it was over one hundred
and fifty. None of the more famous of the
English letter-writers had so large a con-
stituency. The number of Gray's correspondents offers a perfect contrast. But Gray was
fastidious to a fault — a man of fine genius
undoubtedly, but of narrow sympathies, and
purely academic growth. Burns, on the other
hand, was of catholic sympathies, and absolutely

careless in his companionships : all men were, not in theory merely, his brothers. A *Luath* by accident of birth, he had the nature of a *Cæsar*, and, like him, in sheer frankness of disposition, would have " spent an hour caressin' e'en wi' a tinkler gipsy's messan." His correspondents included persons of every social rank, from earls to tradesmen ; and of every degree of culture, from university professors to field-workers. Farmers, sailors, shopkeepers, shoemakers ; military officers, excise officials ; teachers, doctors, clergymen ; lawyers of every grade, from the Dean of Faculty to the humble law-clerk; ladies of titled rank, gentlewomen, and serving-maids; editors, booksellers; bankers, factors, and wine merchants, are all among the number. It is very noticeable that among his correspondents were ladies of superior accomplishments. Four of these received more than one-fourth of his entire published correspondence. His letters to them are the most generally interesting, perhaps, that ever he wrote, and certainly they include his best. His letters to Mrs Dunlop are all good—as Carlyle was the first to observe. She received as many as forty-two. Readers will differ in their estimate of his letters to Mrs M'Lehose ; they will agree in finding them interesting. To this lady he sent forty-eight. Mrs Maria Riddell is accredited with eighteen, and Miss

Peggy Chalmers with eleven. The several characters and dispositions of these ladies, which were in remarkable contrast, are reflected in the general style in which he variously addresses them. He is perfectly at his ease with them all, but he shows the ease which he feels in different ways, apparently adapted to their several dispositions. Mrs Dunlop and Mrs M'Lehose, as revealed in his letters to them, are sense and sensibility personified. With a strong dash of sensibility in her nature, Mrs Maria Riddell has more spirit than Mrs M'Lehose. Miss Peggy Chalmers is piquant, prudent, and modest.

Of his male correspondents the most highly favoured with letters from Burns was George Thomson. He received fifty-six. But it must be remembered that it was less Thomson that was favoured with those letters than the cause he represented. There was much in Thomson's nature that was not in complete harmony with Burns's. The intimacy never ripened. Robert Cleghorn, the farmer at Saughton Mills, near Gorgie, we should imagine, was more a man after the pattern of Burns than Thomson, though to him only nine letters can be set down. An honest, manly heart was the passport to Burns's affectionate liking, and that, with all his coarseness, Cleghorn seemed to possess. Thomson was probably honest-hearted, but he was deficient in manliness—there was an effeminacy or shallow purity in his nature which he could not conceal by the assumption of what he believed to be manly airs. Peter Hill, the bookseller, a seceder from Creech, and the two Edinburgh writers, Robert Ainslie and Alexander Cunningham, were, next to Thomson, with respect to the number of letters they received, the most favoured of Burns's male correspondents. They received sixteen, fifteen, and fourteen respectively. After them comes James Johnston, the printer of the *Musical Museum,* to which Burns contributed; he received thirteen letters. Then follow Commissioner Graham of Fintry, to whom eleven letters; James Burness, of Montrose, Burns's cousin, to whom ten; Cleghorn, already mentioned; William Burns, the poet's younger brother, a saddler by trade, to whom eight letters; Dr Moore, the author of *Zeluco* and other novels, better remembered for his son's sake, the hero of Corunna, to whom eight also; John M'Murdo of Drumlanrig, eight; Richard Brown, a ship captain, to whom seven; Gavin Hamilton and John Ballantine, to whom also seven each; William Nicol, of the Edinburgh High School, to whom six; and, not to exhaust the list, Alison Begbie — supposed to be the *Mary Morison* of the well-known lyric—James Smith, and Robert Aikin, to each of whom five letters. It is rather remarkable that the poet's own relatives should have received so few. The one to his father, a remarkable letter in several ways, is all, perhaps, that we could expect. But there are none to his mother, none to his sisters; and Gilbert, with whom he was on terms of mutual respect and affection, received only three. His wife received but two; there is, however, some explanation to account for the paucity of his letters to her. An uncle, Samuel Brown, was favoured with one—if, indeed, the old man was not rather scandalised with it. And his father-in-law received two, the second little more than a repetition of the first. There is, however, small wonder that the *dour* mason received so few — the wonder is rather that he received so many.

It is hardly wrong to say that Burns knew good English only from books, and practised it only on paper. He was not in the way of hearing it spoken, and he was not in the habit of speaking it. It was comparatively unknown to him as speech. He was never in England to make profitable acquaintance with it as a living language, and the educated Englishman, visiting Scotland, did not often bring the sound of it to his ear. The cultured of his own country, with whom for one brief season he occasionally associated, did not speak it, we may venture to say, as purely as they wrote it—a jealous Englishman might add that they did not always write it quite purely either. Certainly they professed a great belief in English as the distinctive speech of good society, and in their exalted moods rather despised the vernacular as little other than a pagan *patois;* but one has the suspicion that they put on their high English with their company clothes, and found relief and a sense of freedom in putting it off again. Even while allowing that Mackenzie, Stewart, Robertson, Blair, and Greenfield spoke English as well as they wrote it, we may yet venture to believe that Edinburgh society a hundred years ago practised a mode of speech which was no nearer to good English than French of Stratford-atte-Bow to French of Paris. The vocabulary in fashionable use might be mainly English, but Scottish idioms would abound, and the northern accent be all-prevailing.

Whatever the state of "society" language in Edinburgh in 1786-7, the influence of Burns himself was, so far, adverse to the use of English, and in favour of Scottish word and idiom. He came willing to learn of fashionable society the speech of England, and found himself their teacher giving them lessons in the use of their mother-tongue. They listened, applauded, quoted him. He arrested for a time the slow and irregular revolution that was going on in the native speech, and made the native speech temporarily fashionable. His "poems in the Scottish dialect" seasoned the talk of the town. "The language that I had begun to despise as fit for nothing but colloquial vulgarity seemed to be transfigured by the sorcery of genius into the genuine language of poetry. It expressed every idea with a brevity and force, and bent itself to every subject with a pliancy in which the most perfect languages often fail." These were the words of an educated contemporary of Burns, and they expressed the feeling and the judgment of every cultured Scotsman who read the poems.

It is more especially true of the youth of Burns that his knowledge of English was practically and almost solely derived from books. Those who influenced him in the pursuit of this knowledge were his father, his schoolmaster, and a few of his schoolfellows. From none of them could he derive much direct help in the formation of a good style of English composition. His father's conversation, no doubt, stimulated him to a habit of vigorous and independent thought, which was not without its value, but the bent of mind of the elder Burns was towards the exact sciences, amongst which we may include Calvinistic divinity, and turned but little, if at all, towards the elegancies and refinements

of artistic expression. It was with facts and
ideas the old man dealt: words and phrases
were no more to him than the mere wrappers
of thought, to be flung aside on receipt of the
parcel. His hard life seems to have taken all
the poetry, and all the feeling for it, out of his
nature. To the charm of literary grace he was
probably insensible. The influence of the lad
Murdoch upon the education of Burns was considerably more to the purpose. His *method*, so
far as it went, was good. It was enlightened
beyond the general practice of his own and
many a subsequent day. It may be questioned,
indeed, whether the most approved modern
method of dealing with an English classic in
our junior schools is much in advance of
Murdoch's. He taught his pupils to re-arrange
rhetorical inversions in the natural order of
prose, to express the original in a paraphrase of
their own words, and to recite the more poetical
passages. The value of the method, like the
value of a tool, would be, however, in its application. To produce the best results it would
require knowledge, discrimination, and taste in
the teacher. Whether young Murdoch was possessed of these qualifications in any noteworthy
degree may be doubted. It should be remembered that he was only some seventeen or so
when he was engaged by William Burns, in an
hostelry in the town of Ayr, to teach the little

school of five families at Alloway. Under his tuition the boy Robert Burns became acquainted with a large number of English words, stored his memory with numerous quotations, and learned to express himself with fluency. He also learned the rules of grammar, and made such proficiency in the fruitless exercise of *parsing* as to become—so he tells us himself with some self-complacency—quite an adept in "substantives, verbs, and particles" before he was ten. All this schoolboy proficiency had but slight bearing on the art of composition.

The influence of his schoolfellows began after schooldays were over, and was communicated in the course of a correspondence with them on subjects of a literary nature. The lads formed themselves into a kind of Corresponding Essay Club. None of this correspondence has been preserved. It was in full stream when Burns was about seventeen or eighteen. "I kept copies of any of my own letters that pleased me, and a comparison between them and the composition of most of my correspondents flattered my vanity. I carried this whim so far that, though I had not three farthings' worth of business in the world, yet every post brought me as many letters as if I had been a broad plodding son of day-book and ledger." The chief value of this correspondence was the encouragement it gave him to persevere in the

slow and laborious art of English composition,
by convincing him that he was a much superior
letter-writer to any of his correspondents.

In short, the best thing that his school-life
could do for him was to introduce him to
English authors of repute, and leave him to
learn from them. But it is not by the inter-
rupted study of a silent language that a master's
grasp of that language is soon, if at all, to be
attained. The best teacher is the living model;
and constant exercise of tongue and pen, in his
presence, and subject to his correction, is the
natural and speediest means to the acquisition
of a free and fair use of any language. This is
the advantage that most English writers, whom
we regard as classical, have had. It was an
advantage denied to Burns. If his prose be
judged severely on its merits, more than half of
it will be found to be undeniably good, and
much of it excellent English. But let the
deficiencies and disadvantages of his training
receive due emphasis, and the qualities of
force, freedom, and grace in the prose expression of Burns become indeed phenomenal.

The first book to awaken Burns's mind to
a consciousness of style was Mason's " English
Collection." The poet tells us, in the longest as
it is one of the best pieces of his own prose, how
the first bit of English literature to give him
pleasure was the " Vision of Mirza." It was

Addison, too, and not a native author, that was
his first favourite in poetry ; and it is significant
of the religious atmosphere in which he was
bred, that the poem which sounded the earliest
music in his boyish ears was the hymn beginning " How are Thy servants blest, O Lord !"
Addison, then, was the first of the recognised
masters of style to influence the composition of
Burns.   But Addison belonged to a school of
which, if he was not the head master, he was at
least one of the most distinguished representatives.   Of the same school, but with variations
of style which clearly differentiated them from
each other, were Steele, Sterne, Swift, Mackenzie,
Pope, Goldsmith and Shenstone, Thomson and
Young, all of whom were devotedly studied by
Burns, some of them extravagantly admired,
and, especially in the earlier half of his correspondence, rapturously, if somewhat stiffly, imitated.   His reading was not by any means
confined to these authors, but these were his
accepted masters, after whom he moulded his
phrases and modelled his periods.   He was not
alone in regarding them with feelings which,
amounting as they did almost to reverence, are
a great puzzle to the present age.   The universal
feeling at the close of last century was that there
was but one style of prose in the history of
English literature, and that was the style which
is associated with the name of Addison.   There

was no good prose before he wrote, and there could be no good prose in the future that was not shaped on the pattern of his. The English language on its prose side had received its ultimate development; it had no capabilities beyond the point it had reached—fondly believed to be the point of perfection; the forces of nature and art combined could go no further in the composition of artistic English prose. It was the English Augustan age, and as it could never be excelled, the utmost that could be done was to maintain and continue it. Even if he had been an Englishman, with a full native inheritance of the language, it would have been natural for Burns to feel and to be influenced by the prevalent opinion; but, born as he was in a Scottish cottage, a son of the people, and knowing English only at second-hand, and with much of the feeling of a foreigner, it was inevitable that he should be carried away by the general belief that the wits of Queen Anne's reign were the only possible, the imperative models of a classical style of English prose. His desire to imitate them was thus a justifiable one; and the charge of affectation, so often brought against him, falls to the ground. Burns, like his age, consciously followed his models, and made no secret of the imitation. There was no insincerity in his style. He had no other to begin with. As time passed, experience of life and constant exercise in composition purified his style; he became a clever disciple of the Queen Anne School—he was always a respectable one —and was developing a style of his own, specimens of which may stand to his credit alongside the best work of the best English letter-writers, when he was cut off prematurely in the middle of his thirty-eighth year.

The history of his style divides into three, or perhaps four, pretty well defined periods. The first period ends in the spring of 1786. It was the most eventful, the critical year of his life. Previous to this his prose productions were, at best, clever imitations of his models. The next period extends to near the close of the Clarinda correspondence. It is characterised by great inequalities, but gives unmistakable proof— notably in the biographical letter to Dr Moore —that he had now attained to something very like mastery of an expressive, vigorous, and manly style. The Clarinda correspondence gave greater freedom and flexibility to his pen, and, after developing a phase of unusual turgidity of expression, left him in possession of a remarkably clear, pure, and nervous style, of which the following extract will serve as a specimen :—

"When we wish to be economists in happiness, we ought, in the first place, to fix the standard of our own character; and when, on full examination, we know

where we stand and how much ground we occupy, let
us contend for it as property; and those who seem to
doubt or deny us what is justly ours, let us either pity
their prejudices or despise their judgment. I know you
will say this is self-conceit; but I call it self-knowledge.
The one is the over-weening opinion of a fool who fancies
himself to be what he wishes himself to be thought; the
other is the honest justice that a man of sense, who has
thoroughly examined the subject, owes to himself. Without this standard, this column in our own mind, we are
perpetually at the mercy of the petulance, the mistakes,
the prejudices, nay, the very weakness and wickedness of
our fellow-creatures."

The next period includes his frankest letters
—the letters which, upon the whole, show him
at his best as a writer. He is now seldom self-
conscious, writes with a readier pen, and in an
easier and more worthy style. This period goes
down to the time when he first perceived the
shadowy premonitions of ruin, and felt the
hopelessness of averting it. The last is a short
period, in which he wrote little—he had little
heart to write—and put much into small compass. The last letter that he wrote—it was the
last production of his pen — is typical of the
short series which it closes :—

"I returned from sea-bathing quarters to-day. My
medical friends would almost persuade me I am better;
but I think, and feel, that my strength is so gone that the
disorder will prove fatal to me.—Your son-in-law,
"R. B."

The stern, calm bravery, in view of the last enemy, which breathes in this brief note, is in startling contrast to the semi-hysterical sentences which precede our quotation, and which furnish the occasion of the letter.

The discrepancy of opinion pronounced ostensibly on the style of Burns's letters by judges of acknowledged reputation is one of the marvels of our literary criticism. It is, 'perhaps, to a large extent traceable to the insufficient discrimination of the substance of the letters from the style. The critics may be separated into four classes—first, those who declare that all his letters were composed as exercises and for display; second, those who declare that they are the best ever written, and always sympathetic and sincere; third, those who declare that all their blemishes are due to his correspondents, and all their beauties to himself; and last, those who declare that the blemishes are his own, but that they are the exception and not the rule. With the last decision — it is Carlyle's — all kindly readers will, and all candid readers must, agree. It is a remarkable fact that to common people, ignorant of the subtleties of style and unconscious of conventionalism, the letters of Burns are scarcely less interesting than his poetry. It is the matter alone that engages and enchains their attention.

The letters and journals of Burns are interesting in various ways; their chief interest arises from their biographical value. They directly reveal in the familiar light of common day all the main and most of the minor features of his character. They put before us nearly everything of his conduct that we know. Where they do not expressly reveal, they often significantly suggest. They are, in short, the most authentically complete, and therefore the best collection of facts we can possibly have about him. All biographies of him, all criticisms and comments dealing with his motives and actions, must be based upon the testimony of these letters; and must all be referred, for confirmation or confutation of any position they may take up, to the same authority. His letters and journals are a more continuous and communicative guide than his poems; taken along with them, they are the only reliable guide to the heart and life of Burns. They, however, formulate no complete judgment of their author, furnishing only evidence for judgment, and probably on that account are in some danger of being neglected for the rhetorical interpretations and rigid estimates of critics and biographers. The subject of his career is a fertile one, and has been written upon, and written about, till quite a library has arisen around the name of Burns.

M

At least one disadvantage of such a pile of commentaries is that it is apt to hide the subject, the true Burns, from us as behind a barricade of false portraits and fancy sketches. The consequence is that many people indolently take their views of Burns at second-hand, rather than force their way self-reliantly to the source of all information on the subject, and look and judge for themselves.

His poems show Burns at his *extremest*. They exhibit him in his happiest, tenderest, most indignant, most dignified moods. They represent the summits of his life. His ordinary work-a-day range and level are revealed to us in his prose. There we have in a long scarcely broken series of views the man Robert Burns, divested of his singing robes, his laurel crown, and his lyre—handling the rude implements of his earthly toil, and wearing "hodden gray, and a' that." We surprise him at his work, and look in upon him at his leisure. We find him in taverns and at trysting trees. We meet him in the world's ways, in crowded streets, and on the country roads. We accompany him in his few hurried movements, between years of steadfast toil, up and down through Scotland—first from western Ayr eastward to Edinburgh, then northward through Killiecrankie Pass to Cawdor Castle, and finally

southward to where he settles in Dumfries.
At one time he is on foot, at another carried
like a fine gentleman in a Sedan chair; now
he rides in a hired post-chaise with the irascible
Nicol; now, on the back of his mare Jenny
Geddes, he races with a wild John Highland-
man along Loch Lomond. We realise in the
pages of these letters his changing circumstances of scenery and of society. We are
introduced to his friends, hear of his enemies,
have glimpses of his drawing-room admirers
and his pothouse companions, and one delightful
peep at his neutral Nithsdale neighbours. The
last mentioned are rather puzzled with the phenomenon of his poetical presence. "They look
upon me," he writes, half-amused and half-
annoyed, "as if I were a hippopotamus come
to Nithside." We see him in his bachelor
lodgings in town, in his own happy farm-home
at Ellisland with Jean and his children beside
him; we follow him, with his fatal excise-
commission in his pocket, in his unfortunate
migration to the town of Dumfries. We
observe his bearing in the various relations of
life—which in his case are necessarily numerous.
We watch the rise and growth of his sympathies
and raptures; we see his actions; we listen to
his free off-hand remarks, his ever-returning
earnest questionings, his half-formed opinions,
his firm decisions. Above all, we share his

frank confidences on the four great topics of
life, love, politics, and religion.

His letters are not the letters of an ordinary
man.   Still less are they the letters of a
literary man.   There is no class narrowness,
no professional fastidiousness, either in the
subjects with which they are concerned, or
his treatment of them.   The thoughts that
most constantly engage his mind, as their
recurrence year after year in the midst of
transient cares sufficiently testifies, are to be
noted as especially significant of the man.
They are on themes of everlasting human
concern.   They deal with the nature and origin
of man, his rights and responsibilities, his duties
and his destiny.   They are full of regretful
bewilderment at the mystery of suffering, and
the blind awards of fortune ; and are charged
with a feeling of mingled pity and scorn for
the artificial distinctions which tear in sunder
the great brotherhood of mankind.   An earnest
and ever-recurring curiosity in the invisible
destiny of man is a strong feature of the letters.
It runs through all his graver correspondence.
He is certain of the existence of a benevolent
God ; he ardently wishes he were as sure of
the immortality of the human soul.   " Tell us,
ye dead ! will none of you in pity disclose the
secret, what 'tis ye are, and we must shortly
be ? " is the question that turns up periodically

in his letters, and that lies for ever unanswered and for ever a burden in his mind. Jeffrey advanced a strange theory on the subject of the loftier themes of Burns's letters. With what now seems to be a shallow criticism of the letters, he declared that the serious topics were caught out of the air, and thrust into service for mere effect—that Burns might pose as a philosopher ; and further, that this small and unworthy motive was avowed in the apologetic complaint with which Burns frequently prefaced them, stating that he had nothing to write of, and had therefore to hawk about for a subject. The frequent complaint referred to should be easily found—but is not; and as Burns thus gives no support to the statement, we fall back upon the great critic's remaining reason for making the charge, and find it to be that " many of the letters relate neither to facts nor feelings peculiarly connected with the author or his correspondent." But this means no more than that Burns's letters did not fulfil Jeffrey's apparent definition of a letter as a species of com-position which ought to limit itself to ephemeral matters. Jeffrey expected to find Burns's letters to be like the letters of an ordinary man, and because they did not answer his expectations, he accused their author of forcing his subjects, and of affecting sentiments which he did not feel. A continuous and candid study of the

letters will show convincingly that their more
serious subjects, of which they so largely treat,
were not caught out of the air, but out of the
author's mind and heart, where they furnished
matter for his daily contemplation.

The statements of the letters do not always
agree. The writer is not always to be taken at
his word. It would be easy to bring a charge
of inconsistency of opinion against Burns. It
would be easy to bring such an accusation
against any man — those excepted whose
opinions are from the first perfect and infallible.
In what life that is intimately known to us do
we discover no contradictions? Yet, though
they do not agree, the statements are none the
less veracious records of a living and very
pronounced personality. The contradictions
present little difficulty to the formation of a
fair estimate of the essential forces of Burns's
character. It is, however, necessary that he
who would form such an estimate should bring
with him to the task the due qualification of a
nature cognate with that of his subject. It is
only people of like nature that can understand
each other. Enlightened by such a sympathy,
he will know how to handle conflicting evidence.
He will do right to bring to the front what is
expressive of genuine and deep-seated native
sentiment. What is indicative only of the
caprice or passion of the hour he will put in the

background.   He will set everything in proper
perspective.   A novel and Chinesely picturesque
view of Burns will be produced if the process
be reversed—if, that is, what was accidental in
the conduct of Burns be represented as if it
were typical of his nature, and if his really
significant actions and utterances be suppressed
or comparatively ignored.   A false, indeed an
impossible, Burns will be the result of such a
preposterous process.   Yet such a process has
been used, and seems at present to be in some
favour.   One would-be biographer, from a total
want of kindred sympathy with his subject, has
unconsciously adopted it; and it has been
employed to an alarming extent by another,
probably from a desire to say something new
and original on a subject that is still popular
after a hundred years' discussion.   For example,
it has been asserted or implied that Burns never
really loved woman in his life, least of all Jean
Armour, and that his marriage with her made
shipwreck of his happiness and his hopes ; that
he was a kind of rustic Don Juan on principle—
a practised "hawk at the sport" of ruining
women—who could only "batter" himself into
passion ; that religious fervours in such a man
were little better than blasphemous ; that his
passion for Clarinda was mere "philandering,"
yet that this philandering produced the best of
his lyrics ; that his Edinburgh experiences were

already his ruin, before ever his marriage, which is declared to have been the true cause of his ruin, took place ; that the Edinburgh magnates behaved well to him from first to last; that he went to Ellisland a man already exhausted of heart and hope and genius; that he produced during his residence in Dumfriesshire nothing worthy of comparison with the six months' work which formed the contents of his Kilmarnock book; that his songs, although including *Highland Mary*, *To Mary in Heaven*, *Scots Wha Hae*, *A Man's a Man for a' that*, and many others—in short, almost the whole series—were a mere " whittling of cherrystones," and the only literary effort of which his enfeebled mind was capable; that *Tam o' Shanter* is scarcely so worthy of praise as the *Address to a Louse;* that it was by his style, for which he was indebted in a very uncommon degree to Ramsay and Fergusson, and not by his matter that he stormed the world ; and that he died of being Robert Burns in his thirty-seventh year !

These are some of the eccentricities and absurdities of a recent estimate of Burns, almost the only merit of which lies in the literary style in which it is expressed. But probably the writer would be content to have his style praised at the expense of his judgment. In his estimate of Burns we have seen that style is everything, matter nothing—or a very secondary thing indeed. It is surely unnecessary to controvert in detail the quoted positions of his estimate as just summarized. The best of his representation will scarcely stand debate; the most of it is the veriest travesty of the life and character of Burns. Certainly the new and entirely original part of his estimate is a melange of fancies, falsities, and garbled facts. An examination of the only authentic biography of Burns, his own writings, both verse and prose, will make this clear to any person who brings to the study a virile mind and a heart sympathetic with rural scenes and rustic life.

THE FIRST DR HORNBOOK.

THERE were brave men before Homer got hold of Agamemnon ; and there was a Dr Hornbook in Scottish literary history before the discovery, or invention, in 1785, of him of Tarbolton. The invention—for three-fourths invention it was—made in that year by Robert Burns, was a development for artistic purposes of a very respectable mannie, John Wilson by name. This, of course, was not "Wee Johnnie," the Kilmarnock typographer ; though Wilson was equally deserving of the diminutive—at least in respect of height. He developed, however, a breadth of body sufficient to constitute a presence ; with, to complete the portrait, a complacent look, an easy temper, a huge intemperance in snuff, and a pair of bandy-legs habitually presented to the world in black stockings and knee-breeches. " I never could understand why Robbie Burnes took such umbrage at me," he used to say in the pensive moods of his later life; "for we were aye the greatest o' frien's." In hilarious hours, when surrounded with the comforts of the Sautmarket, he would vary the reflection, agreeably to his immediate circumstances and society : " It was a lucky day for me when Rab Burnes fell foul o' the schulemaister o' Tarbolton ;" and the truth is that, while Burns's lampoon shut his shop for him—a little village grocery store, with a supplementary shelf for a few professional drugs ; shut his school too, though more slowly ; and sent him his solitary way from Tarbolton— it was also the beginning of his good fortune. He came to Glasgow, succeeded to the mastership of a school from which his predecessor had been promoted to a University Chair, conjoined with teaching—he had a pluralising habit—the duties of Session-clerk for the district of Gorbals, then a rising suburb; and, being paid proportionately to the number of marriages and births in his district, presently found himself a man of means with a good social position, in which death did at last really surprise him, but at so late a date as January 13, 1839. If the satirist had himself reached that date he would have been within a fortnight of rounding the fourscore.

This was the later, and lesser, Hornbook. His crimes against rustic Ayrshire were limited to over-dosing with salts, senna, and a quack preparation of his own (sc. Hornbook's Mixture) ; to the occasional fractional extraction of a tooth, not seldom the wrong one ; to such simple surgery as bleeding a grazier and blistering a weaver for the same ailment. His crime against Burns was more heinous : he monopolised the talk at a meeting of the local lodge, and aired his acquaintance with " Buchan an' ither chaps " to the admiration and edification of all, and the disgust and disbelief of one. That one vowed inwardly " to nail the self-conceited sot ; " and there, like a " foumart" on a stable-door, he hangs *in terrorem* to all succeeding generations.

But the first and greater Dr Hornbook was discovered in 1507 or 1508 by our earlier Burns, the great, neglected William Dunbar. The circumstance that Dunbar unmasked in metre a Dr Hornbook does not, of course, make him a Burns. It would be Fluellen's reasoning to argue that it did. At the same time there is unquestionably a greater similarity between the " Old Makkar" and the modern poet than ever existed between Monmouth and Macedon. Leaving this for the present, we can authoritatively declare that John Damian, French John, John the Leech, Curly-haired John—whatever epithet, in short, distinguishes him in the State Records of Scotland—was, indeed, a full-blown Dr Hornbook, who, in comparison with the petty huckstering at Tarbolton, did a wholesale business in France and Scotland.

In a foot-note to his poems, Robert Burns

states that the Hornbook of *his* century undertook at his own hand, without the excuse of a
diploma, the three great offices of the medical
art—those, namely, of apothecary, surgeon, and
physician.   The first Dr Hornbook was equally
thoroughgoing in his profession, and far more
sanguinary in his practice.   "In potingary he
wrocht great pine ; he murdered into medicine ;
in leech-craft he was homicide."   His surgical
weapons—his saws and whittles—his "irons,"
as Dunbar calls them—are described with terrific
realism.   They suggest the tools of a torture-
chamber.   They were large and rude as house-
rafters ; with them he operated on a great scale.
He had a large variety in his *garde-de-viande*—
his cupboard.   One can well believe that

> "Where he let blude, it was nae laughter ;"

and that

> · · · "it was nae play,
> The proving of his science."

His pills and potions were proportionate to his
grand style as an operator.   A single dose for a
simple ailment was potent enough to kill "a
wicht horse."

> "His practicks never were put to prief
> But—sudden death, or great mischief."

He did not confine his ravages to one district.
He was a moving terror, who, after depopulation

here, proceeded to extermination other where.
It was in France that he commenced practitioner, having already fled from Italy to escape
inquiry for slaying " a religious man."

> " To be a leech he feign'd him there,
> Whilk mony a man rues evermair ;
> For he left neither sick nor sair
>   Unslain, ere he gaed thence."

It was then that he came to Scotland to " assay
his cunning." The new Palace of Holyrood
opened to receive him and his case of instruments — his unspeakable cupboard. He was
taken into the King's service. Not on James,
however, did he intrude with his awful " irons."
He practised on royalty in other sort. But in
Edinburgh he had rare " carving of vein organs,"
and struck many a " sterving straik." To injury
he added the insult of requiring a large fee :

> " He would have, for ae nicht to bide,
> A hackney and the hurt man's hide,
>   Sae meikle he was of moyens."

That is, his fee for a night's attendance was the
value of a horse, and therewithal his patient's
skin ; so costly a ruffian he was.

Dunbar follows the fortunes of this ancient
Dr Hornbook into the impostures which he
practised on James IV., both as a " multiplier,"
or alchemist, and as " the Freir of Tungland "
in Galloway, and leaves him at last " in a dub

among the dyucks," into which he had fallen in
an unsuccessful attempt to fly from the walls of
Stirling Castle. The satire did not daunt him,
for it did not shake the King's belief in him.
He continued to play "at dice and cartes" with
his Majesty, and down to the fatal year, 1513,
he practised a lucrative imposture as "alchemist
to the King." He had given up the Hornbook
"trade;" there was less money and more risk
in it. Possibly he resumed his original calling
after 1513. In some subsequent year he certainly played a principal part in the real tragedy
of *Death and Dr Hornbook.*

AULD LANG SYNE.

ULD LANG SYNE is popularly known and used as a phrase, a song, and a sentiment. The phrase is a happy one. Burns thought it " exceedingly expressive." It compresses into small and euphonious measure much of that tender recollection of one's youth which, even to middle-aged men, seems to be brought from a very distant but very dear past. On the heart even of a lexicographer it has a lenitive effect, for what saith old Jamieson ? " To a native of this country, it conveys a soothing idea to the mind as recalling the memory of joys that are past." The inventor of the happy expression is unknown. It was already the property of public speech, circu‑ lating freely from mouth to mouth, before anybody thought of tracing it to its parent mouth. The date of its admission into song is conjectural. But its entry into literature may be hazarded with some confidence. To most people this took place on 17th December 1788, when Mrs Dunlop received from Burns a letter in which the following passage occurs :—" Your meeting, which you so well describe, with your old schoolfellow and friend, was truly interesting. Out upon the ways of the world! they spoil these social offspring of the heart. Two veterans of the men of the world would have met with little more heart-workings than two old hacks worn out on the road. *Apropos,* is not the Scots phrase *Auld lang syne* exceedingly expressive ? There is an old song and tune which has often thrilled through my soul. You know I am an enthusiast in old Scots songs. I shall give you the verses." And here follows one version of the popular song known to us, and to all future generations—many may they be!—of patriotic Scotsmen as AULD LANG SYNE. The writer then goes on (with a deception that does not deceive) to express a sentiment which we can devoutly echo, " Light be the turf on the breast of the heaven-inspired poet who composed this glorious fragment! There is more of the fire of native genius in it than in half a dozen " — he might modestly have said half a hundred—" of modern English bacchanalians." Will anybody explain why the national bard towards the close of his too brief career sought not infrequently to pass off as traditional fragments songs that were undoubtedly his own composition ? There is a

N

stanza in his ballad of "Bonnie Jean" which
we think may throw some light on the question.
He asks his correspondent Thomson, of the
well-known *Select Collection*, whether he has not
come across the stanza before, somewhere or
other? The stanza is entirely his own, both
words and imagery, and a beautifully pure
one it is. Did the inspiration of these verses
glide into his mind like a dream, to make
him doubt the reality of their parentage in
himself?

But to return to Auld Lang Syne. Burns's
well-known letter to Mrs Dunlop, with its
precious enclosure, was *not* the first entrance of
Auld Lang Syne into literature. This was
made under the conduct of Francis Sempill—
according to Chambers and Mr Gosse. Sempill
died not later than 1685—the year before the
birth of Allan Ramsay, and the version of Auld
Lang Syne attributed to him opens with the
stanza :—

> " Should auld acquaintance be forgot
>   And never thought upon?
> The flames of love extinguishèd
>   And freely past and gone?
>
> " Is thy kind heart now grown sae cauld
>   In that loving breast o' thine,
> That thou canst never ance reflect
>   On auld lang syne?"

The happy phrase was sure erelong to re-

appear. Ramsay, in 1724, placed it in a song
of his own composition in an early part of the
first volume of his *Tea Table Miscellany*. This
song reappeared in the first volume of Johnson's
Scots Musical Museum, published in the summer
of Burns's sojourn in Edinburgh. Burns was to
contribute many a song to the succeeding
volumes of Johnson, but his annotations on the
songs of the series down to the conclusion of
the fourth volume are not without their interest
even to the general reader. These annotations
were made in an interleaved set of the *Museum*
belonging to Robert Riddell, Esquire of Friars
Carse, the poet's near neighbour and good
friend at Ellisland. The note on Ramsay's
song is as follows :—" Ramsay here, as usual with
him, has taken the idea of the song and the first
line from the old fragment, which will appear
in the Museum, vol. v." The first stanza of
Ramsay's song may be given to illustrate the
remark :—

> " Should auld acquaintance be forgot,
>   Tho' they return with scars?
> These are the noble hero's lot,
>   Obtained in glorious wars.

> " Welcome, my Varo, to my breast ;
>   Thy arms about me twine,
> And make me once again as blest
>   As I was lang syne."

It will be perceived from this specimen stanza

that the song in Ramsay's hands is a true—somewhat voluptuous—love lyric, and not a song of good-fellowship and old friendship, as these expressions are usually understood. But what about the old fragment which Burns promised for Johnson's fifth volume? That volume appeared in the December following the sad event of his death,—which, as Scotland knows, took place in July 1796. And the old fragment was just the song of Auld Lang Syne which he sent to Mrs Dunlop eight years before, and which he had composed at the suggestion of a passage in one of that lady's letters to him. Burns's Auld Lang Syne had one more historical appearance—in the second volume of Thomson's *Select Collection*, published in July 1799. The manuscript was sent to Thomson in September 1793, with the following reference to it, in perhaps the most ponderous letter the poet ever penned:—" The air is but mediocre, but the following song, the old song of the olden times, and which has never been in print, nor even in manuscript, until I took it down from an old man's singing, is enough to recommend any air." There is one important difference between the copy of this song sent to Mrs Dunlop and Johnson, and that sent to Thomson. The difference lies in the order in which the stanzas are arranged. The second verse or stanza, exclusive of the choral verse, of the

Museum is placed last in the *Select Collection.*
That verse goes :—

> " And surely ye'll be your pint stowp !
> And surely I'll be mine !
> And we'll tak' a cup o' kindness yet
> For auld lang syne."

We must confess to a preference for the
arrangement in the *Collection.* Why ? Because
the song is a re-union, and *not* a parting, song
in its very essence. We are aware of the
practice of making it a parting song, and probably he would be a daring man who would
now seek to break a custom that has become
universal, by restoring it to its proper place as
the inaugural song of a festive gathering of old
friends. Does anybody doubt that it is a song
of re-union ? Look at the argument—for even
a lyric has an argument ? " We are old friends,
who have been long parted ; we played together as boys by burnside and on brae ; let us
shake hands, and sit down to a social dram,—
and if it run to a pint, a *Scots* pint, apiece, why,
the occasion is a rare one, and the heartiness of
our waught will prove the heartiness of our
mutual welcome."

As it may not be generally known, we may
here refer to a parody of his serious "Auld
Lang Syne," which exists in Burns's hand-
writing, and is presumably his. It opens
thus :—

" Should auld acquaintance be forgot
  And never thought upon ?
Let's hae a waught o' Malaga
  For auld lang syne."

There are two expressions in Burns's song which, before we quite leave it, may be noticed. The one is "a right gude-willie waught," and the other "gie's a hand o' thine." These are what Burns wrote. It is, however, not uncommon to hear the first given "a right gude-walie waught"—which, indeed, is not without its recommendation to drouthy neibors. "Gude-willie" is, of course, indicative of good-will and kindly feeling ; "a gude-walie waught," again, is a right copious draught. The second has been altered to "gie's a haud o' thine,"—which, for one or two petty reasons, does not seem to be quite so good as the original.

As to the sentiment implied in "Auld Lang Syne," a great deal might be said. As the ministers might say, it is a fertile text. Two points of interest which it suggests may be noticed. In the first place, it makes for nationality. It reminds us of our past history as a people, and encourages the preservation of all that is good in that past. Of course, it pre-supposes a knowledge of Scottish history. *For auld lang syne* is no bad equivalent for the French *prestige*. In the second place, it reminds us of our past as individuals. It tends to the formation of a kindly and consistent character.   There are very few who, slightly to alter Wordsworth, do not wish

> " their years to be
> Bound each to each in natural piety."

The retrospective habit encouraged by the sentiment of "Auld Lang Syne" is likely in most cases to realise the wish.

OUR EARLIER BURNS.

WHEN the poet Crabbe was the guest of Sir Walter Scott in Edinburgh in 1822, his host entertained him one evening by reading specimens of the poetry of the old *Makkar*, William Dunbar. " I see," said Crabbe, " that the Ayrshire ploughman had one giant before him." Scott's own judgment, which proceeded on a vastly more particular knowledge of Dunbar, is more emphatic. He claims for him an equality with Chaucer in respect of " brilliancy of fancy, force of description, power of conveying moral precepts with terseness, and of marking lessons of life with conciseness and energy, quickness of satire, and poignancy of humour ;" he styles him " the excellent poet, unrivalled by any that Scotland ever produced." This belief will help to account for the comparative moderation of Scott's enthusiasm for Burns —a moderation rather implied than expressed. It is almost superfluous to quote the testimony

of other critics. Thomas Warton, the historian
of English poetry, thought Dunbar "the first
poet who had appeared with any degree of
spirit in satirical allegory since Piers Plowman."
Pinkerton anticipated the opinion of Scott by
declaring him the possessor of the best qualities
of the best old English poets. George Ellis
found him "admirable, and full of fancy and
originality as a satirist, a descriptive poet, and
a story-teller; and, in his moral and didactic
pieces, superior to all who preceded him, and to
nearly all who have followed him." He revised
his opinion to strengthen it—finding Dunbar
the greatest poet that Scotland has produced.
Dr Drake accredits him with "first-rate abilities
for humour and comic painting, and an equally
powerful command over the higher regions of
fiction and imagination." Lastly—not to extend
the list of Dunbar's critical admirers unduly—
the late Dr David Laing, who was the first to
correct Dunbar's poems, and whose edition has
not yet been superseded, can find no poet near
our own time whom Dunbar so much resembles
as Robert Burns. Even in this comparison he
has no difficulty in perceiving the pre-eminence
of the elder poet in respect of expressive persona-
tion and allegorical imagery; while "for strength
of satire, richness of humour, vivid description
of external nature, and characteristic delinea-
tions of life and manners, it would be difficult

to say which of these poets is entitled to the higher praise."

With such a series of eulogistic notices by men of rare critical competency before us, we are surely tempted to ask how it happens that the subject of them is so little known. It is no sufficient answer to say that he has only shared the fate that has long overtaken his contemporary, Sir David Lyndsay. The case is that Dunbar has become the victim of a more oblivious fate, and has been infinitely less deserving of it. Nobody has said of Lyndsay what the critics unanimously say in praise of Dunbar. In comparison with Dunbar, indeed, Lyndsay was little more than a mere versifier. He was a reformer rather than a poet,—who for very good reasons preferred verse to prose, urging his reforms in bold and sententious rhyme. His verses in great measure effected their purpose, and the interest in them passed from the popular mind with the occasion that called them forth. Many of Dunbar's themes, on the other hand, are of perennial interest, dealing as they do with those elemental thoughts and feelings which are for ever common to human nature; and even those of them that were incidental to the times when he lived are treated in a manner so truly poetical, that they positively constrain an interest which would otherwise have been withheld. Good poetry, it is true, must be generally

intelligible to be popular; but age and antiquity
of style will not account for the prevalent ignorance of Dunbar among his countrymen of to-day.
His diction is, doubtless, partly obsolete, but his
idioms, when divested of their uncouth spelling,
and especially his directness of expression, come
with a naturalness that is startlingly modern.
Chaucer's period was about a century before
Dunbar's, yet Chaucer's age and antique style
have not proved such obstacles to educated
Englishmen that they fail to appreciate and
enjoy his poetry. How, then, does it happen
that so excellent a poet as Dunbar, less antique
than Chaucer, and in many points his peer, is so
little known in Scotland that even his name is
unfamiliar except to a few? This ignorance is
partly to our reproach; it is partly the result of
an accident. It is to our reproach that as a
nation we give little or no encouragement to
the study of our ancient native authors, the old
Makkars; and it is especially to the reproach
of our Universities that they treat our native
literature, both ancient and modern, throughout
its entire line, with comparative or total neglect.
They have elaborate courses of lectures upon
English literature, wherein they discuss at length
the doggerel of Skelton and the origin of the
sonnet, but they have nothing at all adequate to
say of Dunbar, and take but a meagre notice of
Ramsay, and even Burns. We have one chair

—quite enough!—established for the cultivation, or rather the preservation, of Gaelic;
Scottish literature, which is so much more sib
to the national life, is left to take care of itself.
It may be that when Berlin and Oxford have
included the study of Scottish literature in their
arts' curriculum, Edinburgh or Glasgow will
follow the example! Meanwhile, it is encouraging to know that a German professor, Dr
Schipper by name, has recently published in
Berlin a very creditable edition of William
Dunbar for the use of German philologers.

It is right, however, to say that this reproach
attaches only to this and, in a less degree, the
preceding generation. For it is only fifty years
since the collected Works of Dunbar were placed
before the public. The statement is a remarkable one. Here we have an excellent poet, who
flourished towards the end of the fifteenth and
at the beginning of the sixteenth century, who
was eminently popular in his lifetime, and
acknowledged by his contemporary brethren to
be their leader, or one of their leaders, yet whose
works were collected and published for the first
time so late as 1834. Now and again in the
century preceding this date, a few specimens of
his art were included in various collections of
ancient poetry, Allan Ramsay initiating the
series in 1724 in the well-known *Evergreen*.
For the two centuries before that again, Dunbar

and his Works lay buried in oblivion. His
poems ceased to be read, his name ceased to be
mentioned, his influence was lost. The unhappy
fatality of Flodden, with its disastrous and far-
reaching consequences, was mortal to the fame
and influence which he had already created.
That fame and that influence lost the momentum
which in other circumstances they would justly
have acquired. They lost the momentum of
two centuries. When his poems were discovered in 1724, and at last collected and published in 1834, Dunbar was virtually a new poet,
speaking a language no longer quite intelligible,
and without a living tradition of fame to recommend him. The discovery has charmed scholars
and critics, but he has not yet been found by
the people of Scotland. Is it impossible to
introduce him? This will depend very much
upon the manner of the introduction. He has
been so long absent from his native land that,
now he is returned, he looks like a foreigner,
and we think we can never be familiar with him,
nor he with us. His garb is outlandish; his
accent, if not his words, is foreign. But let us
overlook his garb, and forget his accent, and we
shall make discovery that he is with us in heart
and soul and sentiment. A true human heart
beats under that outlandish dress; true Scottish
sentiments are uttered in that foreign accent.
And, after all, the dress and the accent are not

foreign; it is the old Scottish dress and accent
such as our forefathers used four centuries ago.
To some those antique forms are no bar, but
rather a charm, to intercourse with the old
Makkar; they need be no bar to our Universities, where Homer and Horace are studied
in their native and original guise. But if unfamiliar spelling and the occasional use of an
old-world word keep the mass of the people
from knowing William Dunbar as an honour to
his native land and a power for good in Scotland,
I for one see no sin in translating his poetry into
the form and vernacular of to-day. It would be
difficult to do this well. It would be comparatively easy to do it so as to attain the desired
object. The experiment of modernising an old
Makkar was made in the case of Blind Harry, a
contemporary of Dunbar. His epic of "Wallace" came strongly recommended by its subject
to the heart of every Scotsman, prince and
peasant alike, and in equal measure to each;
and survived the century so perilous to Scottish
literature and art—the fateful sixteenth century.
The momentum the nation gave it sent it down
to smoother times; but it was losing its popularity because of the increasing uncouthness of
its form and phraseology, when a translation of
it, in 1722, into the current vernacular, revived
its interest and gave it a fresh lease of life,
which has expired only in the present century.

Now, that translation, which was the work of Hamilton of Gilbertfield, the friend and correspondent of Allan Ramsay, was wretched in the extreme. It was nearly as bad as it could be. It was a paraphrase which all but failed to preserve any spark of the fire, any breath of the spirit of the original. And yet it was successful ; and it continued to be so as long as it was to be had. It was immensely popular among the peasantry for three generations. It fed the patriotism of Scotland for a hundred years. It was the bosom-friend of young Burns, who knew Blind Harry in no other form, and who caught the patriotic flame which so burned in his soul, and so blazed in his immortal war-ode, from *its* feeble fire. If, by merely modernising the form of the Minstrel's "Wallace," with scarcely an attempt to retain the spirit of it, such results were produced, I venture to think that a careful modernised version of William Dunbar would do something—would do more, perhaps, than any other agency—to revive the fame of the ancient bard with whom fate has dealt so unkindly, and to restore to Scotland an influence long, unhappily, lost to the country.

Fortune has been very unkind to William Dunbar. He dropped from public notice pretty early in the sixteenth century, and remained unnoticed for about two hundred years. Political agitations, affecting the very existence of the State, followed by ecclesiastical revolutions of the most sweeping character—all, perhaps, remotely traceable to the accident at Flodden— passed in successive storms over unhappy Scotland in the sixteenth century. Those commotions did good—did harm; they wrought many changes in the national institutions, customs, and accomplishments, and even in the national character. We were a gayer people before they began; and though our gaiety often ran to extravagantly licentious lengths, it allowed and encouraged that freedom without which true art, whatever the material in which it works, cannot thrive. But political independence and religious liberty are of first and foremost concern to a nation. To them every other interest must give way. And in Scotland the interests of literature in nearly all its departments, of music and architecture, of what one may call social accomplishments, were to a disastrous extent swept aside in the civil and stern religious strifes of the sixteenth century. Amongst those strifes the poems of William Dunbar disappeared. By the rarest accident, almost unique in the chronicles of literature, they were not for ever engulfed and forgotten. Such a fate overwhelmed some of his contemporaries, and might have been his. It may be as well here to enumerate the Scottish *makkars* of the fifteenth century who were contemporary with

Dunbar. Dunbar himself will furnish the list.
They were Maister John Clerk, James Afflek or
Auchinleck, Holland, Sir Mungo Lockhart of
the Lee, Clerk of Tranent, Sir Gilbert Hay,
Blind Harry, Sandy Traill, Patrick Johnstoun,
Merser, Roull of Aberdeen, his namesake of
Corstorphine, Brown, Maister Robert Henryson,
Sir John the Ross, Stobo—described as " guid
and gentle " (his real name was Reid)—Quentin
Shaw, and Maister Walter Kennedy. To this
list add the names of Gavin Douglas and Sir
David Lyndsay. How few of these are familiar
names to-day ! Some of them are nothing but
names, and probably never now can be anything
else. *Nomen et umbra sumus* is their brief record
and elegy. Of the poetical compositions, famous
in their day, of quite half of them, not a line, or
only the veriest fragments, have been found.
They perished in the storms of the sixteenth
century. It was not their fate to perish because
they were little admired in their day, or less
commended than the scarcely less unfortunate
survivors. The worst of Kennedy, the great
Ayrshire poet before Burns, the lad of Carrick
as Burns was the lad of Kyle, has been discovered ; his best is lost. Of Quentin Shaw,
who was also of Ayrshire, only one production
is known to exist. Yet these two poets were
regarded by Lyndsay as worthy to be called
great ; and Gavin Douglas thought them the

O

only rivals of Dunbar, and placed them with him in the "Muses' Court" in his own poem "The Palace of Honour."

The way in which Dunbar's poems—such of them as we have—so narrowly escaped annihilation is interesting enough to be told. That some, if not all of them, were printed in his lifetime cannot be doubted. It is at least known that eight of his pieces—"The Golden Targe," "The Flyting with Kennedy," "The Twa Married Women and the Widow," "The Lament for the Makkars," "The Ballad of Kittock," "The Testament of Andro Kennedy," "The Ballad of Lord d'Aubigny," and a ballad fragment beginning "In all our garden grows there noo nae flow'r"—were printed and published in the first book that ever came from the Scottish press. This was the well-known press of Chapman & Myllar, and the date was 1508. Of this book only one poor mutilated copy exists. It was found in 1788 in a private library in Ayrshire, and may now be seen in the Advocates' Library, Edinburgh. What became of the rest, and of the subsequent editions, if any? Those which accidental fire and the fires of invasion may have spared, their own popularity, by frequent use, may have destroyed. Be that as it may, if we had only black-letter to depend on for Dunbar's poems, we should have had no more than those eight specimens of his

poetical genius.   MS. is the forlorn hope where
print fails.   But forlorn hopes are sometimes
realised, and, strangely enough, the fame of
Dunbar was for the most part in the frail
tenure of two MSS. till the eighteenth century.
It happened that Sir Richard Maitland of
Lethington, in East Lothian, relieved the cares
of high public office by collecting or selecting
specimens of his country's poetry, apparently
for his own amusement and use.   This was a
little past the middle of the sixteenth century.
About the same time—more particularly for
three plague months in 1568—a Mr George
Bannatyne had set himself the same congenial
task.   Bannatyne's MS. is preserved in the
Advocates' Library, Edinburgh, and contains
at least fifty-one pieces of Dunbar's composition (*i.e.*, generally attributed by critics to
Dunbar).   Maitland's is in the library of Mag-
dalen College, Cambridge, and contains a good
proportion of the works of Dunbar, including a
score or so which are not to be found anywhere else.   So far as we possess them—but
it does not follow, by any means, that we do
possess them all—Dunbar's collected poems,
as last published (in 1883-4-5, by the Scottish
Text Society), include one hundred and one
pieces, of which ninety are certainly the composition of Dunbar, the rest being more or
less probably his.   They have been collected,

in the proportion named, from the following sources :—

8 from Chapman & Myllar's Black-letter Volume of 1508 ;

51 from Bannatyne's MS. of 1568 ;

27 from Maitland's, compiled about the same time ;

9 from Reidpeth's MS., written in 1623 ;

2 from Asloane's MS. of 1515 ;

3 from MSS. in the British Museum ; and

1 from the second volume of the Register of Sasines in the Town Clerk's Office, Aberdeen.

Of these, the Bannatyne MS. is the most famous as well as the fullest. It was the first to reveal to present times something of the vigour and versatility of the old *makkar*. The MS. lay long in the house of Sir James Foulis, of Colinton, near Edinburgh; it was put into the somewhat unscrupulous hands of *honest* Allan by a friend of the Foulis Family, and in 1724—rather more than a century and a half after it was written—it supplied a large proportion of the two volumes of Ramsay's "Evergreen," and, as Dr Irving puts it, "not only helped to revive a taste for vernacular poetry, but directed the attention of better antiquaries than Ramsay to Bannatyne's precious collection."

We have dwelt thus far on the unanimous

testimony of competent critics to the extraordinary merits of Dunbar's poetry, and on the
perilous adventures of two centuries through
which his poetry passed, in order to excite some
curiosity in the man William 'Dunbar, and to
awaken an interest in his work. To the student
an interest in the man will probably follow an
acquaintance with the poet. You can hardly
read his poetry without feeling that he was a
man well worth knowing. It gives you the impression that, excellent though the poetry is, it
does not by any means present all, or even the
best, that was in him. The best of Burns, it has
been said, died with him; it was in his face, his
figure, his conversation. A glance, a gesture, a
remark, was often more eloquent, more thrilling,
than anything he has written. You think it
must have been so with Dunbar. From his
naturalness, ease, sincerity, sustained force, and
versatility, you have the feeling that he was
greater and ampler than his published poetry—
that, in short, poetry was not with him only the
expression of an occasional mood, but of a
habitual condition. He seems to have breathed
a poetical atmosphere. Unfortunately, we can
now know very little that is absolutely definite
about his external life. The place and date of
his birth and his family connections are largely
conjectural. His work and wanderings are
obscure. His personal appearance, manner,

and habits are merely hinted. None of his
letters are preserved ; no portion of his conversation is recorded. The place and time and
circumstances of his death have not been directly
determined. And yet, though the portrait is a
blurred one, though the figure is far off and
fugitive, though the story of his life exhibits
many gaps, it is possible by close attention to
known facts, and by careful inference from them,
to create to ourselves some image of the poet's
personality. A good many of his poems are
autobiographical, but rather of his inner than of
his outer life. In these we form quick and intimate acquaintance with the essential nature, the
character and disposition, of Dunbar ; but the
information they incidentally afford of his outward life and circumstances is scanty in a
tantalising way. They presuppose your possession of full particulars. Yet it is from his own
poems that most of our knowledge of his personal history is derivable. A foreign State paper
or two, the Treasurer's Accounts of the Household Expenses of James IV., and some contemporary verse, furnish their meagre but sometimes
significant quota : and with the information thus
obtained, it seems, we must be content.

Dunbar was born probably not later than
1460, and almost certainly in Lothian. The
biographers who assign his birthplace to the
village of Salton have been misled by a mistake

of Allan Ramsay. Sufficient for Salton the fame of Andrew Fletcher and his one saying. In all probability, however, Dunbar came from East Lothian. That he was connected with the March branch of the once-powerful family of Dunbar cannot be doubted, but the degree of the connection is undecided. The late Dr David Laing conjectures that he may have been the grandson of Sir Patrick Dunbar of Beill, in the county of Haddington. In the once notorious *Flyting*-match between Dunbar and his western rival Kennedy, the latter, searching about for material of abuse, upbraided Dunbar with the evil deeds of his ancestors. He reminded him how his " forebear," Corspatrick, Earl of March, was a traitor to his country, the ally of Edward Longshanks, and the enemy and reviler of William Wallace. However reduced were the circumstances of the parents of Dunbar, they were at least able to give him a good education. St Andrews, the oldest of our Scottish Universities, was then also the foremost in learning and science. Hither young Dunbar was sent when he was about fifteen or sixteen years of age, presumably in the year 1475. At least his name is in the list of Bachelors of Arts for the year 1477, and this degree could not be taken till after two years' study at the University. He took a full course, and commenced *Master* in 1479. In virtue of this latter degree he is

uniformly designated—according to the custom
of those times—*Maister* William Dunbar.　We
know comparatively little about the early condition of the Scottish Universities, but it is at
least known that, when Dunbar was a student,
St Andrews was the envied possessor of an
unusually good library, and benefited greatly
from the literary patronage of the resident
Archbishop, William Schevez.　One is curious
to know the course of study required at the old
Universities, and in one of his later poems,
entitled " Learning Vain without Guid Life,"
Dunbar in a general way partly satisfies the
curiosity.　Logic, we learn, was a prime subject
of study; rhetoric was carefully cultivated;
natural philosophy, as it is still called, was
expounded in the old approved Aristotelian
method; astrology was taught; and, in addition, there was the study of poetry, juris-
prudence, and theology.　It would seem that
Dunbar was destined for the Church from his
infancy.　On his nurse's knee he was dandled
as " little bishop."　It is known that he was employed in Scotland, England, France, and elsewhere, as a preaching friar of the Order of St
Francis.　It is quite possible that he entered
upon, and completed, his novitiate in the Grey-
friars' Convent, then recently established in
Edinburgh.　There he would be more fully
instructed in philosophy and divinity, and in

the rules and requirements of his Order. He
entered this Order when still young ; but he
may previously have visited Paris, like many
young Scottish graduates of his time, to prose-
cute his studies at the famous University there.
Dunbar, in becoming a Grey Friar, may have
made a virtue of a necessity. At all events, he
appears to have possessed the great qualification
of absolute poverty demanded of all the brethren
of the Order. The other Orders, familiarly
known to us from the colour of their habits as
Black Friars and White Friars, were required to
despise wealth, but might still hold property : it
was the distinctive feature of the system of religious life and work founded by St Francis that
those who adopted it should practise absolute
poverty. They could own no property ; even
the gown, the cord, the shoes they wore, were
not their own. Dunbar, then, became a mendicant friar ; and by and by we get an occasional
glimpse of him in his patched cloak, and with
his scrip and his clam-shells, preaching and
begging his way through Lowland Scotland,
and in England, and even as far as Picardy in
France. A great object of his preaching was
the suppression of the heresy of Lollardism.
He had many adventures and experiences, not
all honourable or even honest, and not all un-
holy either. He was eminently sociable, full of
humour, and fond of fun, yet with pensive moods

and seasons of pure and tender devotion. His
hymn on the Passion of Christ, with its tender
refrain, " Oh, Mankind, for the Love of Thee,"
was doubtless the production of one of his
devout moods. The opening verse represents
him entering an oratory, fasting and fatigued
with his journey, kneeling down with the suffer-
ings of God in his memory, and suddenly falling into a slumber, in which he witnessed all
the sad scenes of the Divine Tragedy. This
poem is sufficient to prove that, if he preached
as he wrote, his sermons must have been instinct
with vivid description and unaffected pathos.
The life of a holy friar, however, had its un-
holy side. It would hardly be fair to accept
Kennedy's representation of it, as exemplified
in the life of Dunbar, without making liberal
allowance for the licence of ink and poetical ingenuity. This, however, is Kennedy's account :—

" Fra Ettrick forest southward to Dumfries,
    Thou beggit as a pardoner through the kirks ;
Collops and curds, meal, groats, an' grice, an' geese,
    And, i' the dark, thou stole ev'n staigs an' stirks—
    So that braid Scotland wi' thy begging irks."

But Dunbar himself has left on record his
general experiences in the grey garb :—

" My fortune was to be a freer,
The date thereof is past this mony a year,
    But within every pleasant toun an' place
    In England a', fra Berwick to Calàce,
I have within the habit made gude cheer.

" In the freer's habit have I aften fleecht,
  In it I have in pulpits gone and preacht,
    In Dernton Kirk, and eke in Canterbury ;
    In it I passed at Dover ower the ferry
  To Picardy, an' there the people teacht.
  As lang as I did bear the freer's style
  In me, Gude kens, was mony a wicked wile,
    In me was falsehood every wight to flatter ;
    That could be washed oot with nae haly watter ;
  I was aye ready a' men to beguile."

It will readily be inferred from this confession
that Dunbar at last, and apparently pretty early
in his career as a friar, abandoned the Order as
unsuitable to his disposition. He found that he
could not get on without stooping to practise
flattery, falsehood, and deception. He found
that he had not been a servant of St Francis
at all, but of a fiend in the likeness of St
Francis. Yet his life as a wandering friar,
bringing him into contact with many different
scenes and much and varied society, must have
strengthened and stored his mind with the
materials of poetical thought. From under that
gray hood a pair of observant eyes, the busy
servants of an active and thoughtful brain,
were quietly taking those views of nature and
human nature which his verses yet express so
freshly because so truly. Nor must it be forgotten that the profession itself, of which he
was a member, and with whose tricks and tradi-
tions he was necessarily well acquainted, gave

him the material for themes which might be treated satirically, or humorously, or morally, according to the mood of the moment. Dunbar was certainly well qualified by personal knowledge to write such a tale as the " Freirs of Berwick." And probably the " Table of Confession " is a solemn record of the shortcomings and trespasses of the Brotherhood.

Dunbar was somewhere between twenty and thirty when he abandoned the itinerant life of a friar for the scarcely less roving life of an Embassy Clerk. The phase of life upon which he then entered was no less likely to be useful to him as a poet. How the connection came to be made is not definitely known, but there is abundance of proof to show that he was on several occasions on the Continent in the diplomatic service either of the King or of the King's agents. There can be no doubt he was employed in the capacity of a clerk. Learning, especially the ability to compose and write, was in those days almost exclusively the accomplishment of the clergy, at the same time that it was indispensable in the diplomatic service to the maintenance and extension of friendly relations with foreign States. Years afterwards, when his wandering days seemed to be over, and he hung about Edinburgh in loose attendance upon the Court of James IV., he made occasional reference, in many a rhyming petition to the King,

to his long faithfulness and zeal in the foreign
service of Scotland. "My youth," he said,
"was spent with pain and grief in your service."
"It is a painful thing," he said, "to reflect that
all my labour and service, so loyally rendered,
is little better than lost; I have tarried long
and waited humbly, and my recompense is of
the smallest." And again, "It is not only that
my service at home is forgotten, but my service
in the neighbouring countries of France, England, Ireland, and Germany, and in the remoter
lands of Italy and Spain as well." And once
he reminds the King that his very fidelity to
Scotland kept him poor, for in his youth he
had received offers abroad for the use of his
pen :—

> "When I was young and in guid ply (*plight*),
>   And would cast capers to the sky,
>   I had been bocht in realms near by,
>   Had I consentit to be sauld."

It is, however, from Kennedy's vituperative
attack upon Dunbar that fullest information is
to be had of the geographical range of Dunbar's
services. The notorious "Flyting" match furnished Kennedy with the valuable occasion.
That Dunbar provoked the attack is undeniable.
He wrote Sir John Ross that Kennedy had
a very great opinion of himself; that he had
not, however, dared to express that contempt of

his contemporaries with which doubtless he presumptuously regarded them ; but that, if he had done so, he would have found more than his match to reckon with in the person of him, William Dunbar, the writer of the letter. In a kind of *postscript* he declares that it would really give him pleasure if Kennedy had the courage to slander him ; it would raise the devil in him, and he would rhyme the slanderer into ridicule in every country in Christendom. There can scarcely be a doubt that Dunbar intended Ross to show Kennedy the letter. That he did show it, the event proved, for Kennedy presently penned a short but sufficiently scurrilous reply. Thus began an altercation which would have horrified Menalcas and Damœtas. Dunbar answered at great length, and with a vigour of vituperation and a profusion of rough and ready rhymes that showed his heart was in the work. The least objectionable part of the answer may be given because of the ridiculous light in which it humorously presents his opponent, and the picturesque side glimpse it affords of the streets of Edinburgh four centuries ago. Kennedy, who belonged to Ayrshire, and was the son of a Scottish nobleman, held an appointment which required his occasional presence in the capital. Dunbar pictures his arrival at the West Port, and his reception in the High Street :—

" Thou brings the Carrick clay to Enbrugh cross,
　Hobblin' on buits that are as hard as horn ;
Strae-wisps stick oot whaur that the walts are worn ;
　Come thou again to scar' us wi' thy straes,
We shall gar skell oor schules a' thee to scorn,
　An' stane thee up the causey whaur thou gaes !

" At Edinbrugh the bairns like bees oot-thraws,
　Cryin' lood oot, ' Here comes oor ain queer clark ; '
Then flees thou, like a hoolet chased by craws,
　While at thy buit-heels a' the toun tykes bark ;
Then cry the wives ' Look whaur the rascal gaes ! '
　Anither cries ' I see he wants a sark,
I rede ye, cummer, tak in your linen claes ! '

" Then rins thou doun the gate, with noise of boys,
　An' a' the toun tykes hingin' at thy heels ;
Of lads an' loons there rises sic a noise,
　Auld aivers tak the road wi' rattlin' wheels ;
　An' cadger pownies cast baith coils an' creels
For noise o' thee, an' rattlin' o' thy buits :
　Fishwives cry ' Fie ! ' an' fling doun skills an' skeels,
Some clash at thee, some clod thee on the cuits ! "

Kennedy rejoins in a letter that runs to three
hundred lines, and is charged with the utmost
licence of language. It is abuse run mad. There
is nothing in Dunbar's life, person, parentage,
or profession, capable of being turned to his
disgrace, of which Kennedy does not take extravagant advantage. The Scottish dictionary,
copious as it was in abusive epithets, seems to
be literally exhausted of its resources to over-
whelm Dunbar. It will hardly be believed, that
after all, and indeed all the while, Dunbar and
Kennedy were the fastest of friends, who loved

and admired each other all the more for the
mastery of scurrilous verse which they severally
displayed, and who had only undertaken a
mutual satirical assault for their own pleasure
and the amusement of their countrymen.

The " Flyting " match between Dunbar and
Kennedy has many points of interest, not the
least important of which is the revelation it
affords of Dunbar's history. It is unnecessary
here to quote the passages which furnish this
revelation : it will be sufficient to notice that
Dunbar, on the authority of Kennedy, was in
France on the King's Commission, that he had
gone thither on board the *Katherine* (probably
with the Earl of Bothwell, Ambassador to
France in 1491), that he had been sick on the
voyage, that he spent a winter in Paris, waiting
to cross the Alps to Italy in spring; that on
another occasion he sailed from Leith and was
driven by storm to the coast of the Netherlands,
northward past Denmark, past Norway, and at
last shipwrecked on the coast of Zealand, where,
"barefoot and breekless," he begged from door
to door, crying in Latin, " Charity, for the love
of God ! "   King James IV.'s relations with
foreign courts are matter of history. He kept
up constant communication with a number of
European States, especially France, Spain,
Flanders, and Denmark. He made his influence
felt in those countries as a princely and en-

lightened patron of every scholarly accomplishment and knightly art. Soldiers and courtiers,
scholars and men of science, poets and musicians were attracted to his court from abroad,
as well as encouraged at home. His embassies
were conducted by men well qualified to represent the enterprising and liberal spirit of their
Sovereign. Dunbar was certainly one of these,
though he was employed in a humble capacity.
His name, it is true, never once occurs in the
State Records which notice the foreign intercourse of King James. But it was customary
to give only the leading names of the Embassy;
and the testimony of his own verses, as well as
of Kennedy's, sufficiently proves his connection
with diplomatic missions on the Continent.

At last, somewhere near the very end of the
fifteenth century, Dunbar ceased to wander, and
settled—as far as he can be said to have settled
at all—in Edinburgh. He never again acted as
Embassy-clerk, at least on the Continent. He
became Court Laureate, and was known in
London as the Rhymer of Scotland. He was
pensioned in 1500, and kept by the King in
more or less constant attendance at the new
Palace of Holyrood till the fatal year 1513.
The pension was only £10 a year to begin
with; but it rose to £20 in 1507; and in 1510
it was £80. The Privy Seal Register, still
preserved, appoints his pension of £80 to be

P

paid to him at Martinmas and Whitsunday, out
of the King's coffers, by the Treasurer, until he
should be promoted to a benefice worth not less
than £100. He was still a clergyman, though
he had long doffed the regular for the secular
garb. To get that benefice was one of the
desires of Dunbar's life. They read his petitions in a wrong light who see nothing in them
but proofs of the King's neglect and the writer's
discontent. So far from neglecting the poet,
the King was desirous to keep him at court as
much as possible. It would have been easy for
James to grant Dunbar the benefice upon which
he had so set his hopes. But the royal disposition and genius were of a kind to appreciate the
conversational and poetical talents of Dunbar;
and it is very obvious that an unusually close
intimacy existed between the King and the
poet. Even if Dunbar's intimacy with the King
had been less than it was, he had yet influential
friends at court who would have prevailed upon
the King to grant the poet's modest enough
though oft-repeated request, if the King's great
wish had not been *not* to lose sight and service
of Dunbar. Dunbar's desire to get fairly settled
in life was natural enough, especially in one who
was now middle-aged, who had had more than
a full share of active life, and who was well able
to realise in his mind the insecurity of courts
and kingly favour.

His petitions to the King for the reward of a
benefice form an interesting feature of his poetry.
The glorious privilege of being independent was
probably never experienced by Dunbar in the
way he wanted.   It was impossible that the
King could take any offence at those petitions:
they must have amused him—they amuse us.
One can imagine the King smiling at the ingenuity with which the poet renewed his request,
ordering an increase of pension or a present,
and telling him with his own gracious lips that
he valued him too much to part with him.   On
one occasion the petition ran :—

> "Nane can remove my malady
> Sae weel's yersel, sir, verily ;
>   For with a benefice ye may prieve
> Whether I mend not hastily.
>
> "In youth upon my nurse's knee,
> 'Twas *Dandely, Bishop! dandelee!*
>   An' noo that age begins to grieve,
> A simple vicar I canna be !
>
> "Jock, that was wont to herd the stirks,
> Can noo draw till 'im rowth o' kirks ;
>   He hides a fause card up his sleeve,
> Worth a' my sangs aneath the birks."

Another time he urges his request in the humorous character of an old grey horse :—

> "It's I've been lang left i' the field
> On pasture that's baith plain an' peel'd ;
>   I might be noo ta'en in for eild !

My mane—it's lyart noo, or white ;
An' thereof ye have a' the wyte :
When ither horse hae bran to bite
    I get but girss ! "

It was a vain, though a clever, artifice to feign
the King's favourable reply :—

" According to our mandate, gar
    Bring in this grey horse, auld Dunbar,
Wha, in my aucht, in service true,
    To lyart changèd is in hue ;
Gar house him noo, against the Yule,
    An' busk him like a bishop's mule ;
For with my hand I have indost
    To pay whate'er his trappin's cost."

After long waiting, he begged again :—

" I know not how affairs are guidit,
    But kirks are hardly fair dividit ;
Some men hae seven, and I—not ane !

" I ken it is for me providit,
    But, then, sae tiresome 'tis to bide it—
It breaks my heart, an' blunts my brain.

" Great kirks are no' for me to gaither ;
    Ae kirk wad do—tho' roofed wi' heather !
For I o' little wad be fain."

Still the long looked-for benefice did not come ;
and at last the poet, being a man of humour,
found consolation in the reflection that, if he
did not command success, at least he deserved
it. And there was some satisfaction in letting

the King know that. "You have, sir," he says in his remonstrance, "many servants and officers—

"Kirkmen, coort-men, craftsmen fine,
Doctors of law and medicine—

besides jugglers, rhetoricians, philosophers, astrologers, artists, men of arms, and valiant knights; dancers, French-flingers, musicians, menstrils, merry singers, carvers, carpenters—

"Masons building on the land,
And shipwrights hewing on the strand;

printers also, and painters, goldsmiths and coiners, lapidaries and apothecaries,

"All cunning of their craft, and slee,
And labouring all at ance for thee."

Then he proceeds :—

"But tho' that I, amang the lave,
Unworthy be a place to have,
Or in their nummer to be tauld—
Langer in mind my wark shall hauld !
Hailler in every circumstance
In matter, form, and firm substance ;
Not wearing like *their* works away
With rust, or canker, or decay,
But lasting out their labours all—
Altho' my recompense be small !"

Scarcely a greater mistake could be made than to imagine from the Petitions of Dunbar that he was a discontented man from whom all

the pleasures of life had fled.   On the contrary,
he took a proper share in all the festivities and
amusements of the Scottish Court, which was
in the early years of the sixteenth century as
gay as any in Europe, and probably more pro-
digal in proportion to its wealth.   This is matter
of fair and direct inference from his poems.
Their vivid side-glimpses (revealing picturesque
incidents and life-like portraits) of the Court,
fashionable society, and life among the bur-
gesses of Edinburgh, are of the utmost value to
the historian of the reign of the Fourth James,
quite independently of the artistic grace with
which they are presented.   We are present at
a comical dance at Holyrood ; we make the
acquaintance of James Doig, the gigantic keeper
of the Royal wardrobe ; we hear of fools in their
parti-coloured clothes ; black-a-moors arrive at
Leith to fill menial offices at Court ; flatterers
besiege the King's door ; lady solicitors, successful in their petitions, frequent the courts ;
honest country yeomen depart, disappointed in
theirs ; gallant soldiers, like old Lord Bernard
Stewart, create a stir in the town on their
arrival ; New Year's Day is enlivened with pre-
sentations and salutations ; Royal intrigues and
other fashionable scandal are whispered about ;
impudent adventurers, like the Italian quack
who was made Abbot of Tungland, are discussed ; and there is the continual bustle of

feasts and plays and grand processions. Into the spirit of the social life of his time Dunbar fully entered; he danced in the Queen's chamber till he lost a shoe; he ridiculed the surly Doig, and then he soothed him, in verses that must have been equally amusing to the courtiers; he satirised the flatterers, and exposed the adventurers; he unfolded female duplicity, and he fell in love with "Beauty and her twa fair een;" he cried up one town, and he decried another; he went to salute the King on New Year's Day; he took part in the plays; he welcomed the honoured guests of the King; he described the Royal processions; he advised people with money to use it in their lifetime; he preached and practised the doctrine that it was best to be blithe; and he sang that lightness of heart was better than heaviness of purse. He had his graver moods, which, however, at no time deepened into misanthropy; a large fund of native humour, of the kindly and contemplative kind, kept him from despair. And even from the oppressive gloom of gathering years, solitariness, and sickness, he recovered with a brave elasticity of spirits that was as much due to reason as to instinct.

Two incidents that broke the agreeable monotony of his life at Court deserve special notice. The first of these was the marriage of James IV. to Margaret, daughter of Henry VII. of England.

It is extremely interesting to know that Dunbar was one of the notaries dispatched by the Scottish King to England to arrange this marriage. The Embassy was headed by the Archbishop of Glasgow and the Earl of Bothwell, and included a retinue of attendants and followers — Dunbar among them — to the number of about one hundred in all. They arrived in London in October 1501. Their mission, as is well known, was successful, and the English Princess was solemnly affianced at St Paul's Cross in the first month of 1502. In the Christmas week preceding, the chief members of the Embassy were entertained at a banquet given by the Lord Mayor, and on this occasion a poem by Dunbar in praise of London was sung, and so highly esteemed that a present of about £7 was sent to the poet by the ordinarily parsimonious King Henry. And the present was doubled within a week after. The Princess did not come to Scotland till August 1503. Meanwhile, Dunbar had been composing his great poem, "The Thrissil and the Rose," in honour of the approaching marriage; and there can be no doubt that from his first introduction to Margaret's notice, when she was little more than thirteen years of age, down to the unhappy disaster of 1513, Dunbar had a sincere and sympathetic interest in the fortunes of the young Queen. Margaret was quick to observe and appreciate his tender loyalty, and became the poet's warm patroness—"his advocat baith fair an' sweet." If Dunbar's preferment had lain with her, there was probably scarcely a benefice in Scotland to which, when it fell vacant, she would not have promoted him. Dunbar knew this right well, and in one of his petitions he earnestly wishes that the King had been "Joan Thamson's Man"—that is, had been more amenable to the influence of his wife.

> " Sir, for your grace, baith nicht an' day,
> Richt heartily on my knees I pray,
> With a' the fervour that I can,
> That ye were ance Joan Thamson's man !
>
> " For, were it sae, then weel were me ;
> Without a kirk I wouldna be ;
> A' my hard fate were endit than,
> Gif ye were but Joan Thamson's man !
>
> " Oh wad some ruth within you rest
> For sake of her, fairest an' best
> In Britain, since its time began !
> Oh that ye were Joan Thamson's man !
>
> " For it wad harm in nae degree
> That ane, sae fair an' gude as she,
> Sic honour, thro' her merit, wan
> As to mak' you Joan Thamson's man ! "

Dunbar composed several pieces in commendation of "the meek white rose," some of which have the true lyrical lift and movement; and in May 1511 he accompanied her on a progress through the country. northward to Aberdeen, and described the magnificent public reception accorded to her by the inhabitants of the northern burgh. His description, which is clearly that of an eye-witness, includes a notice of a mystery-play or pageant enacted in the streets before the newly-arrived Queen. The Town Council registers show that such dramatic performances were of common occurrence till a gloomy Calvinism forbade them as sinful exhibitions. If the same narrow views of art had prevailed in England, the Elizabethan drama, which rose out of less favouring circumstances than existed in Scotland in the earlier reign of James IV., could not possibly have developed.

With this visit in the Queen's retinue to Aberdeen the public life of Dunbar, as far as it is definitely known, comes to an end. He went on, however, drawing his pension at the half-yearly terms till May 1513. Those terms never came too soon. For Dunbar, from some cause or other, probably from his own liberality and generosity of life, was always impecunious.

> " I canna tell you *how* it's spendit,
>   But weel-a-wat the money's endit."

Again—

> " To reckon up my rents an roums
>   I dinna need to tire my thoums."

Fortunately the Lord Treasurer was punctual.

The poet could depend on him to the day. He celebrates with almost boyish delight the return of pay-day and the punctual Treasurer :—

> " I thocht it lang till *ane* cam' hame,
>   Fra whom I fain wad kindness claim ;
>   His name, sae sweet, I will declare—
>   Welcome, my ain Lord Treasurér !

> " Owre every man, excepp the King,
>   Excepp the Croun, owre everything,
>   Wi' a' my micht, though it was mair,
>   Welcome, my ain Lord Treasurér !

> " Ye keep your tryst sae wonder weel,
>   I haud ye true as ony steel ;
>   Needs nane your payment to despair—
>   Welcome, my ain Lord Treasurér !

> " I had been deep in dumps and dool,
>   Had I wantit my wage till Yule ;
>   But noo I sing with heart *un*-sair—
>   Welcome, my ain Lord Treasurér !

> " Welcome, my benefice an' my rent,
>   The livelihood the King has lent ;
>   Welcome, my pension most preclair—
>   Welcome, my ain Lord Treasurér !

> " Welcome, as heartily as I can,
>   My ain dear maister, to your man,
>   And to your servant evermair—
>   Welcome, my ain Lord Treasurér ! "

Dunbar disappears in 1513. He received his last payment on 14th May. What became of him is unknown. The probability is that he accompanied the King to Flodden, and fell

with him there. If he did, he was not the
only ecclesiastic who attended James on that
fatal expedition. The King's own eldest son
was a victim. Dunbar's name occurs in
no subsequent State paper. The Treasurer's
accounts, it is true, between 1513 and 1515
have been lost; but there is no reference to him
in those that continue the record of the Royal
expenses after the latter date. Neither is there
reference to him as alive after 1513 in any
other document. The inference, drawn from
the staid and sober spirit of his moral poems,
that he lived till he was an old man, is untrust-
worthy; it is the prerogative of genius alike
to anticipate the wisdom of age and to recall
the feeling and freshness of youth. And,
besides, Dunbar was at least fifty-three years
old in 1513—an age which was then, and at a
much later period, reckoned old. Shakespeare,
a century later, complained of being old at
forty. The only objection to the extreme
probability that Dunbar perished at Flodden is
to be found in the three poems which have
been attributed to him, one beginning—

"O, lusty flower of youth, benign and sweet;"

another entitled " An Orisoun, when the Gover-
nor passed into France;" and the third entitled
" The Lords of Scotland to the Governor of
France." The first of these is supposed to be

an address to the Queen-Dowager, but it would fit the case of any young lady who had recently been left a widow. It is certainly Dunbar's, but it may as well have been composed before the fatal day in 1513 as after. The second undoubtedly refers to the departure of the Duke of Albany from Scotland in 1517, but there is doubt of the authorship of it. "It is quite possible," says David Laing, "that this poem, which occurs only in one MS., may have been ascribed to Dunbar by mistake." As for the third poem, it is anonymous. Whoever wrote it must have been alive in 1520. Those who favour the theory that Dunbar was alive then have no difficulty in ascribing it to him. It is needless to argue the point much further. Only this may be said, that if Dunbar was not at Flodden, or if he escaped from it, there is no doubt that the widowed Queen, now that she had the power, would have by-and-by found for him the benefice for which he had long had her good wishes; and there is little doubt that if he had got the benefice, some record of the appointment would have existed. Finally, if his life did not terminate in 1513, it is a remarkable thing that his poetry did.

A survey, necessarily rapid, of the poetry of Dunbar may now be taken. And, first, with respect to his place in literary history, and the sources of his inspiration, he stands half-way between the time of Chaucer and that of Shakespeare, and of the poets in the intervening period of two centuries he is worthiest of mention. Chaucer was his acknowledged master at the outset. To his influence we owe the richly descriptive, if somewhat conventional, allegorical poem of " The Thrissil and the Rose," and the still more ornate " Golden Targe." Chaucer's methods, too, are visible in the vivid characterisation and bold satire—licentious in its freedom—of " The Twa Merrit Women and the Wedo," as well as in the richly humorous and skilfully-conducted tale of " The White Friars of Berwick." These are imitations ; but seldom are more successful imitations produced ; they equal the originals. Another external influence, clearly discernible on the art of Dunbar, is traceable to the hymns of the Church. With these Dunbar as a clergyman was early familiar; and there was much both in their general sentiment and in the solemn airs to which they were chanted to waken sympathetic echoes within him. To this influence we owe such sweetly serious pieces as " The Passion of Christ," " The Table of Confession," " Ane Ballat of our Ladye," and the general strain of " The Lament for the Makkars," with its soul-haunting refrain—derived from the Service for the Dead —" The fear of death's disturbing me." A few stanzas of the last, slightly modernised, may be given :—

> " Our pleasance here is all vain glory,
>   This false world is but transitory ;
>   The flesh is brittle, the fiend is slee—
>   *Timor mortis conturbat me !*
>
> " The state of man doth change and vary,
>   Now sound, now sick, now blythe, now sorry,
>   Now dancing merry, now like to dee—
>   *Timor mortis conturbat me !*
>
> " No state on earth here standeth siccar ;
>   As in the wind's blast waves the wicker, [willow]
>   So waves this warld's vanitie—
>   *Timor mortis conturbat me !*"

Then follows a list of over twenty dead poets, most of whom had been his contemporaries; and then—

> " Since Death has a' my brethren ta'en,
>   He will not lat me live alane ;
>   Perforce I maun his next prey be—
>   The fear of Death is haunting me !"

Dunbar's genius was uncommonly vivacious. He was a poet of many moods. Nobody will deny him the possession of a profound sense of the mysteries of religion, and of the impressive ceremonial in which his Church robed and presented them ; but he could also, in his gayer moods, daringly burlesque the most hallowed forms of the Church service. His macaronics— such as " Andro Kennedy's Testament "—are

clever and amusing, and not without a spice of
legitimate satire to warrant their existence ; but
it is not in the ordinary religious mind to excuse
the reckless, the rejoicing profanity of the
" Dirigé to the King at Stirling." Burns's
" Holy Fair" is saintly beside it. It matches
" Holy Willie's Prayer," but is without the excuse of that hatred of hypocrisy which impelled
the utterance of Burns. It is not satire, but
profane fun.

In the third place there was no doubt the
influence of contemporary Scottish poets. The
extent of this influence it is now impossible
accurately to measure. The works of his contemporaries have perished wholesale. But as
Dunbar was confessedly a leader among them,
it follows that he rather communicated than
received influence.

There remains a substantial body of poems
which must be set down to the credit of Dunbar,
as original, in the strict sense of the word.
These deal largely, but not exclusively, with
personal experiences. They describe the world
in its daily changing relations to the writer, and
especially they convey the undisguised and
genuine thoughts and feelings of his mind and
soul as affected by these relations. Some of
them are satirical, some descriptive, some lyrical,
some laudatory, and a large proportion are
didactic. They include his " Amends to the

Tailors and Souters" (whom he had overwhelmed with ridicule); his history of the hypocritical "Friar of Tungland" (the Dr Hornbook of his day); his Devil's Walk (with an eye to business) among the Trades of Edinburgh, which Dunbar calls the "Devil's Inquest;" his songs in praise of female youth and beauty; his account of the grand doings at Aberdeen on the occasion of Queen Margaret's visit; his various petitions, notably that of the "Gray Horse—Auld Dunbar;" his noble eulogy of London, the "A Per Se" of cities; his generous eulogy of the old chevalier, Lord Bernard Stewart, whom Dunbar may have seen interred at Corstorphine; his "Dream" and his "Headache," with their Heine-like touches; his "Twa Drouthy Cummers," encouraging each other at the fireside of a forenoon, in their husbands' absence, "to fill fu' the glass an' drink;" his description of the busy, noisy, unsavoury High Street of Edinburgh; and, best of all, his "Meditation in Winter." This last is a fine poem, full of a tender, almost a tearful, sympathy with life and nature. It opens with a description of dark and drumlie days. The gloom of a Scottish winter so oppresses him that he has no heart for song or ballad. He cannot sleep at night, but turns and tosses restlessly through the long dark hours. His spirit shrinks within him at the sound of wind and hail and heavy showers driving past his window in the darkness. He thinks, like Burns in "The Vision," upon his desolate and dependent condition. What a poor bargain he has driven with the world! Yet he will not despair. He will hold Hope and Truth fast to the end, and let Fortune work forth her unreasonable rage. Prudence and Age come to comfort him :—

> " Prudence in my ear says aye—
> ' Why wouldst thou have what must away ?
>   Or crave what thou canst have no space,
>   Thou tending to another place,
>   A journey going every day ?'
>
> " And then says Age—' My friend, come near,
>   And be not strange, I thee requere ;
>   Come, brother ! by the hand me tak' ;
>   Remember thou has count to mak'
>   Of all the time thou spendit here.' "

Death comes, not to terrify, perhaps, but to disturb him :—

> " Syne Death casts up his yetts sae wide,
>   Saying—' Thir open shall ye bide !
>   Albe't that thou were never sae stout,
>   Under this lintel shalt thou lout ;
>   There is nane ither way beside !' "

—a Blake-like image! His mortality haunts him, as it haunted Charles Lamb, in winter. No New Year's festivities " may lat [hinder] me to remember this." The concluding stanza is characteristic :—

> " Yet when the night begins to short,
>   It does my spirit some part comfòrt
>   Of thought opprest with winter show'rs:
>   Come, lusty Summer ! with thy flow'rs,
>   That I may live in some disport."

Dunbar wrote in two languages, Scots and English ; for (it seems necessary to point it out) there was a Scottish language in literature before Allan Ramsay wrote the " Gentle Shepherd." He had thus the range of two dictionaries, and he wielded their power with the skill that comes of familiar acquaintance. He knew the fine phrases of fashionable society, and the broad Doric of the villages and farms ; the artificial rhetoric of the old romances, and the realistic slang of the streets. He kept the vernacular for homely subjects treated in a broadly humorous style ; but, like Burns, he used both languages freely in his best pieces, according to the nature of the sentiment he was about to express. Like " The King's Quhair," his English pieces are in the Chaucerian style, which continued to be a model for our native poets down to the Reformation period. After that (it was a long time after) our native poets sought English culture at the feet of French art. The Reformers, in the barren interval, managed to keep Shakespeare out of Scotland. He had no influence on the northern Makkars. As for the people, they never got a chance of feeling the charm, the magic of his genius.

Dunbar's poetical forms deserve some notice. They are unusually varied. He uses the alliterative verse of old English—best known to us in the "Vision of Piers Plowman"—and the heroic couplet of plain narrative, copiously and with a master's ease. But he employs also many measures, or forms of verse, no longer in use, which might well be revived. The rhythm of his stanza is suggestive ; and the rhymes, upon which Dunbar rests for much of his effect, are often bewildering in their easy abundance, and furnish a musical accompaniment not unlike the recurrent tinkle of unobtrusive bells. It is noticeable that he has none of those forms with which we associate the numbers of Burns, and for which Burns was indebted immediately to Ramsay and Fergusson. The influence of Dunbar's genius never reached Burns. " The Evergreen " did not bring their spirits together. Yet the two poets, with important differences, some of them in Dunbar's favour, had several characteristics in common. It must, however, be remembered that Dunbar was our earlier Burns rather because of his general pre-eminence than because of any striking similarity of his genius to that of Burns. They exhibit, then, the same extensive variety of themes, and find them in

the same quarter—at their feet, around them,
in their daily experiences. They have the same
wild flights of imagination, the same versatility
of mood, the same quick recovery, the same
unexpected, daring, and yet delightful transi-
tions. They are equally vigorous satirists,
without having their hearts soured to the legitimate joys of life by a selfish misanthropy or an
egotistical cynicism; they inculcate the same
brave, cheerful, sensible philosophy, and formulate it in maxims of similar terseness, at the
same time that they have full knowledge of
the pathos and tragedy of human life. They
reveal themselves unreservedly, in their inmost
strength and weakness, and neither lose the
respect nor rise beyond the reach of common
humanity. They have the same contempt for
mere extrinsic value in comparison with native
worth; they put the heart above the head, and
both above the purse. As artists in verse, they
show the same keen appreciation of the charms
—which with them, in the language of Burns,
includes " *a'* the shows and forms "—of external
nature, often catching them in a single happy
word or phrase; but they subordinate scenery
to society, nature to man. They exhibit the
same cunning in the conduct of a tale; revel in
the same thoroughly healthy and wholesome
humour, which will occasionally offend the fastidious in morals and the ceremonious in religion;

and are delicately susceptible, but in unequal degrees, to the joy of loveliness in female face or summer landscape. It is inexpedient here to establish or illustrate these positions by quotations from Dunbar. Enough that it can be done, and that we really have in William Dunbar a great poet, well worthy to be called our earlier, and ill deserving to be a neglected Burns.

THE END.

GLOSSARY.

Aiblins, possibly.
Airts, points of the compass.
Aiver, work-horse.
Apple-ringie, southernwood.
Arles, earnest-money.
Atweel, indeed.
Awmous, alms.

Bane, bone.
Bap, roll of bread.
Barley-fever, craving for whisky.
Beas', beasts, cattle.
Bedesman, one who prays for another.
Ben, cottage-parlour.
Bent, grassy wilderness.
Beuk, book.
Bing, heap.
Black-bonnet, elder.
Bonnet-laird, small landed proprietor.
Bothy, ploughmen's hut.
Bood, behoved.
Boortree, elder-tree.
Bracken, fern.
Brae, slope.
Brodd, board or plate.

Braws, finery.
Brose, a mixture of oatmeal and boiling water.
Buchts, bunches (of ribbons).
Buik, bulk or body.
Burrowstoun, burgh.
But, cottage-kitchen.

Ca', drive.
Canny, quiet.
Carse, rich alluvial land.
Caup, cup, bowl.
Change-house, public-house, inn.
Chield, young fellow.
Chop, shop.
Coal-riddle, (plaid) checked.
Cowp, capsize, overturn.
Commonty, a common.
Cookit, appeared and disappeared by turns.
Creuzie, oil-lamp.
Crowdie, a mixture of oatmeal and cold water.
Cruckit, crooked.
Cruive, pigsty.
Crummie, common name for a cow.

Cuist, cast.
Cuits, ankles.

Dandering, wandering.
Dauds, lumps.
Dichtin', winnowing, cleaning.
Dirdum, brunt.
Douce, staid and quiet.
Drouthy, thirsty.
Duddy, ragged.

Eild, old age.
Eldritch, ghastly, weird.

Farl, a kind of cake.
Forby, in addition.
Forbears, ancestors.
Freem'd, strange, strangers.
Fu', drunk.

Gaberlunzie, a beggar.
Gade, gaed, went.
Gae 'wa', go away.
Gang, go.
Gash, sagacious.
Gaun, going.
Geizened, warped with drought.
Glower, stare.
Gowpen, handful.
Greymashes, gaiters.

Haddin', holding.
Halflin, youth.
Hallan-wa', partition at door-way.
Hankie, handkerchief.
Hap, covering.
Harn, coarse linen.

Harnished, harnessed.
Haugh, alluvial land.
Hirsel, herd or flock.
Hoddin', hobbling, jogging.
Hogscore, a line across the ice in curling beyond which the stone must pass.
Hostin', coughing.
Howdie, midwife.
Hurlie, small cart.

Izzat, letter Z.

Jennies, country girls.
Jockies, country lads.
Jeroboam, big whisky-bottle.

Kailyaird, kitchen-garden.
Kaim, comb.
Kintra, country.
Kye, cows.

Labour, (a croft) to till.
Laigh, low.
Laft, loft.
Lamiter, a cripple.
Lattin', letting.
Lay, a weaver's beam.
Letter-gae, precentor.
Lettern, precentor's desk.
Ley, fallow land.
Lippie, fourth part of a peck.
Lint, flax.
Lown, quiet.
Lumhead, chimney-top.
Lucky, goodwife.

Makkar, poet.

Mucked, cleansed.
Mutches, close white caps.

Neibor, neighbour.
Nowte, cattle.

Orra, odd, superfluous.

Paitricks, partridges.
Peeble, agate, pebble.

Quate, quiet.

Rant, uproarious song.
Redd, to put in order.
Rigs, ridges, a set of furrows.
Rink, the curling path.
Ruifs, roofs.

Sark, shirt.
Sclate-stanes, slate-stones.
Scoogs, shelters.
Shanksnaigie, afoot.
Shaws, woods.
Shilpit, meagre, pinched.
Sile, soil.
Siller, money, silver.
Skelping, rattling.
Smytrie, a small collection.
Soo, sow.
Soopit, swept.
Speel, climb.

Stour, dust.
Stow, steal.
Swankie, young vigorous fellow.
Swite, sweat.

Taft, farm.
Tewels, tools.
Thack-an'-rape, thatch and rope.
Thirlage, bond or custom by which the corn of certain lands had to be ground at a certain mill.
Thrang, *throng*, busy.
Thrawn, twisted.
Thretty, thirty.
Toom, empty.
Tryst, a fair, an engagement.
Twal, twelve.

Walloped, flapped.
Wee, little.
Weans, young ones, young children.
Weirdless, regardless.
Wersh, insipid.
Whang, slice.
Whaup, curlew.
Wiel, a pool.
Wizened, withered.

Yill-caup, ale-mug.
Yowt, shout.

Printed by M'FARLANE & ERSKINE, *Edinburgh.*

www.ingramcontent.com/pod-product-compliance
Lightning Source LLC
Chambersburg PA
CBHW031359020726
47499CB00005B/1458